"Will you look at that?" Lola said, amazed. "I think this boy's been hobbled."

Hobbled is an old-fashioned way of confining a horse by tying his front legs together. It's cheaper than fences, but you don't see it, not here.

Except that I *had* seen it before, at a farm about eight miles away. I had seen a horse do exactly what this guy, Noel, was doing. It had been a horse who was the very same color, too.

It wasn't anything I wanted to think about, but I couldn't stop the images from rolling once they had begun.

The horse, legs bent just this way, grazing.

And a few hours later, the horse flat on the ground, dead.

One of Louanne Perry's horses.

It was the reason Noel had looked familiar when I'd first seen him yesterday. Because he was the dead horse resurrected. Oh, God.

"What's the matter with you?" Lola said. "You look as though you've seen a ghost."

I smiled wanly.

I had . . .

By Carolyn Banks

TART TALES: Elegant Erotic Stories
PATCHWORK
THE GIRLS ON THE ROW
THE DARKROOM
MR. RIGHT
THE ADVENTURES OF RUNCIBLE SPOON
THE HORSE LOVER'S GUIDE TO TEXAS (coauthor)
A LOVING VOICE: A Caregiver's Book of Read-Aloud Stories for the Elderly (coeditor)
A LOVING VOICE II: A Caregiver's Book of More Read-Aloud Stories for the Elderly (coeditor)
DEATH BY DRESSAGE*
GROOMED FOR DEATH*
MURDER WELL-BRED*
DEATH ON THE DIAGONAL*
A HORSE TO DIE FOR*

**Published by Fawcett Books*

A HORSE TO DIE FOR

Carolyn Banks

FAWCETT GOLD MEDAL • NEW YORK

A Fawcett Gold Medal Book
Published by Ballantine Books
 Published in the United States by Ballantine Books, a division of Random House, Inc., New York, and simultaneously in Canada by Random House of Canada Limited, Toronto.

http://www.randomhouse.com

Library of Congress Catalog Card Number: 96-96763

ISBN: 0-449-14969-2

Manufactured in the United States of America

First Edition: December 1996

10 9 8 7 6 5 4 3 2 1

For Davis McAuley
who is Jeet-like,
right down to his home fried potatoes

I want to thank my veterinarian, Elroy Whitworth, for his patience as well as his advice. I also want to thank Staci Layne Wilson for her help with the California section, and Davis McAuley and Elisa Wares for reading this manuscript so carefully and guiding me through some very important revisions.

CHAPTER 1

"Wait until you see this guy," said Lola, my best friend. She was pulling a semidressed me across my front porch and out into the yard. "No kidding. He's to die for."

She wasn't talking about a man, of course. She was talking about a horse. But if you know Lo and me, you've probably guessed that already.

I couldn't understand what the big deal could be. I mean, there are a steady procession of horses moving through Lola's life and barn. Buying, selling, rehabilitating. That's the way she makes her living. So this horse, I thought, must really be something.

Still, I wanted to put socks on and brush my teeth—and at least run a comb through my hair first.

Lola *tsk*ed and consented to let me do those things, but she wasn't happy about it. She fidgeted while I performed some cursory morning ablutions.

God. It was barely daylight and I hadn't even awakened my husband yet. I could hear him in the bedroom, snoring softly.

I gargled and spit. "So where'd you get this horse?" I asked her. "And what's the big deal?"

"He's a Christmas present," Lola answered. "From Cody."

"Hmmph," I replied. Involuntarily.

Cody was Lola's live-in beau. Together, he and Lola ran LoCo Farms. Or at least pretended to. Because actually, except for the start-up money, it was Lola's operation all the way. Cody, as far as I was concerned, didn't know a heck of a lot about horses.

Oh, he could ride a little, which was more than Jeet could. But he rode inelegantly, elbows jutting out, hands too high and jiggling. Plus the horses he liked were the ones who had names like Alpo and Sparkplug. I sort of said all this with my next remark, which was, "Great. I can't wait to be dragged out of the house in the middle of the night, practically, to see a horse that Cody would pick."

You remember in those old, old movies, when men would say to women, "You're beautiful when you're mad"? Well, that was true of Lola, who could probably have been a high-fashion model if she'd chosen to pursue that line of work.

Lo rose to Cody's defense, kind of sniffing and making herself taller. "This is a fabulous horse," she said, little rouge-red circles appearing on the cheeks of her fair face. "That's why I want you to see him. Or wanted you to." She swiveled so that she could stalk toward the stairwell.

"Oh, hey. Come on," I said, grabbing her sleeve. "I was just kid—"

"No, you weren't kidding," she said.

"Well, what am I supposed to do?" I asked her. "Pretend?"

"Why do you have it in for Cody?" Lola asked.

"He's got his faults, sure, but you know that I love him."

I sighed. What was I going to say? That I hadn't really forgiven him for what he did to Lola when he'd slept with Nika Ballinger? And on the very same night of his and Lola's engagement party?

No. Lola had to be too awfully aware of his lapse every single minute of her life.

"I get along with Cody just fine," I said. And it was true, sort of. I mean, Jeet and I spent time with Cody and Lo. A lot of time. It was just that I couldn't ever see me really relaxing around him. Really thinking of him as someone good for Lola.

"Cut him some slack," Lola went on. "You can't go around holding a grudge. And anyway, you're going to love this horse."

I wrung a washcloth out and ran it over my face. I didn't bother to use the comb. Instead I let Lola lead the way downstairs, lest our bickering awaken Jeet. He had another hour or so before he had to make his way into Austin for his job at the paper.

We went outside and stood there for a minute, absorbing the moist but balmy atmosphere. "God," I said, softening with the breeze. "It's hard to believe that it's practically Christmas."

"Six more days," Lola said.

That's the way winters are here: mild. When the temperature drops to freezing, which it does sometimes, we all bitch and moan and feel inordinately sorry for ourselves. Meanwhile, friends up North wrote us annually about the unimaginable: snowdrifts and freezing rain—and we'd pretty much ignore their complaints. Or worse. Sometimes we'd insensitively counter them with remarks about how we'd had to run the air conditioner the day before, December something.

Of course, we make up for it in the summertime, when the heat is fierce and unrelenting. And for some reason, that was when most of our horse shows were held: summertime.

"So if this horse is your Christmas present," I said, "how come you have it already?"

"I guess Cody didn't want to waste money boarding him somewhere for a couple of days. I don't know. But I don't care, either," Lola said. "Now, come on."

"I probably should wake Jeet up," I said. "And I probably ought to grain." I'd thrown hay to Plum and Spier, but I usually didn't grain until I'd downed a cup of coffee. Which I'd have done by now if Lola hadn't come barging in.

"You'll be back in a minute," Lola said. "Why can't you do all that when you get back?"

Listening to us, you'd have thought we were annoyed with each other, but we weren't. We always talked this way. I thought of it as sisterly, though neither Lo nor I had siblings.

Still, our mode of conversing made people who didn't know us raise their brows. Because Texas is the South, after all, and in the South, you are nothing if not polite.

My vet, Len Reasoner, was continually trying to teach me Southern ways. So far, his instruction hadn't taken, and I was glad. I hate taking fifteen minutes to get to the point. I mean, who has the time? Lo, however, could be as Southern as all get out with anyone but me. Which I guess was good. I mean, I'd seen Lo, and, indeed, a lot of Southerners, turn manners into a veritable weapon, a way of keeping folks at bay.

I opened the door to Lola's Suburban and lifted all of the junk off the front seat—magazines, an empty Snapple bottle, and about eight of those red cardboard wrappers from McDonald's large fries.

I glared at Lola, who was a head taller than I was, and slender, too.

"What's the matter?" she asked, noting my expression.

"Nothing," I said.

Nothing worth complaining about. Because it wasn't Lo's fault that she could eat junk food all day long and never gain weight. I, on the other hand, could probably weigh two pounds more an hour just by being in the vicinity of a McDonald's wrapper.

Life was so unfair.

"God, you really are in a piss-poor mood," Lola observed. "Remind me never to bother you again before you've had your coffee."

"Coffee would have helped," I acknowledged.

And then we both sort of laughed, remembering dozens of horse shows we'd been to together, horse shows were everybody grumped around some indoor stabling area measuring grain and filling water buckets while the smell of fresh-perked rose steadily in the background. Fifteen minutes later, Styrofoam cups and maybe even a doughnut in hand, the smiles and the good mornings would be genuine, whereas before . . .

Piggo—that's the nickname we had for Lola's vehicle—jerked to a halt, snapping me out of my reverie.

It took less than five minutes by road to get to

Lola's. Usually she and I take a shortcut either on foot or on horseback through the woods. Our properties, her LoCo Farms and Jeet's and my Primrose Farm—are right next door to each other.

"Look," she said, pointing.

But I'd already seen.

Three horses were silhouetted against the new-risen sun in the pasture. A low fog swirled at their feet. Spots of dew glimmered like tossed jewels on the branches of the trees in the foreground.

We sat there for a moment, savoring.

Lo came out of the stall and into the aisle of the barn with a halter on her new horse.

He was all atwitter, head and neck raised, still viewing his surroundings as new. As a result, he looked even taller than his seventeen hands. Indeed, Lo, beside him, seemed tiny.

She was beaming up at him, stroking his neck. He snorted, and Lola laughed as she wiped the product of said snort off her face with her sleeve. Lola handed the lead rope to me, then snapped the cross ties into place.

The horse waited, expecting, I supposed, to be groomed.

"What did Cody do?" I asked, as I moved around him, touching him as I did so. "Rob a series of 7-Elevens?" Because one 7-Eleven wouldn't have been enough to buy a horse like this.

Lola said, "It gets even better. Wait until you see him move."

"Really," I persisted. "Where'd Cody get him? Because, I don't know. I just have this feeling . . . "

It was a vague sense of recognition. You know

what I mean. A niggling sense that I wasn't seeing this horse for the very first time.

"He's from out of state," Lo said.

"It's his color, I guess," I decided.

Technically the color is brown, which, I know, sounds very untechnical. In fact, if you tell people a horse is brown, they'll assume that you don't know squat. Because the horse colors we're familiar with, the colors that most horses are, are known as bay or chestnut (or sorrel, if you ride western).

But brown is a bonafide color.

It means that the horse looks black, but doesn't have a black muzzle, which is what determines true black. If a horse is black and has brown hairs on his muzzle, he's brown.

If you don't believe me, check your Pony Club manual.

Except that what is happening is this: People are too embarrassed to say brown, because they're afraid that word will mark them as a neophyte. And if there's anything a neophyte doesn't want to appear to be, it's what he/she is. So they say, these days, *brown bay*.

But believe me, this horse was brown. And brown is a color you don't see too often.

But it wasn't color alone. It was the overall picture, the *gestalt*. Something . . . something . . .

But Lola and I didn't get into that. Instead, I watched her bring a longe line out of the tack room and snap it to his halter. Then she led him to the round pen, and I followed.

I know what you're thinking. That Lola shouldn't be longeing him that way. That she should have put a longeing cavesson or a bridle on him, then a saddle or a surcingle and side reins.

Except that Lola wasn't interested in longeing the horse for real. To actually train him or ready him to be ridden. She was just showing him off to me. And so she was taking a shortcut here.

I watched his walk as Lola and he moved toward the round pen. They suited each other, I thought. His strides, like Lo's beside him, were long and free.

I leaned on the metal rail of the pen and waited.

The horse had been in a stall, so, of course, Lola walked him for a while. But when she asked for the trot, he didn't take any iffy steps, any steps that were short or tight or mincy. No. He was out there moving as if he were in side reins, you know, pushing out from under himself and arching his neck, trotting with so much float that it didn't seem he was touching the ground at all.

"See?" Lola said, asking the horse to halt. "Eat your heart out."

"Do I get to see his canter?"

"I know what you're thinking," Lola said, asking the horse to walk on, then trot again.

What I was thinking, of course, was how *had* Cody—who wasn't filthy rich after all—afforded such a horse? Unless he didn't have a canter at all.

But the horse did have a canter, and a very nice one at that. "Okay," I conceded, "what's the catch?" Because a horse like this, bare minimum, would have cost about thirty thousand dollars.

"There is one," Lo said. A little frown formed on her face.

"And. . . ?" I coaxed.

"Out in the pasture," Lola said, gesturing beyond

the little enclosures that adjoined most of her stalls, "he charges. Big time. Like the cavalry, Cody says."

I looked up at the horse and tried to imagine the half ton or so that his bulk represented—hurtling toward me. He seemed so good-natured that I couldn't picture it happening.

"It's nothing I can't deal with," Lola said cheerfully, pulling a carrot out of her pocket and letting the horse scarf it up out of the palm of her hand.

And I believed her. She'd handled plenty of bad actors in the past. And she'd turned them, as she liked to phrase it, into useful citizens, too.

"So Merry Christmas," I said, giving her present an appreciative pat.

CHAPTER 2

It was the newly arisen Jeet who had to listen to me raving about the horse, however. He sat there, bleary-eyed, staring into his empty maroon mug as though he'd forgotten the words to the spell that would fill it with steaming black brew.

Usually, you see, I grind the beans and ready everything the night before. Then, as I ease out of bed to see to my equines, I flip the switch that starts the coffee maker.

By the time Spier and Plum have been hayed, I'm back in the house and at least one cup is ready.

When Jeet wakes up there are five cups more, and the morning paper, too, which I go to the end of the driveway to fetch.

So I'm not so bad as a wife.

Defensive, maybe, but not so bad.

This morning, however, Lola had interrupted my routine. And so, while Jeet waited and the pot made sounds remarkably like regurgitation, I babbled.

"He's gorgeous," I said about the horse. "But he charges. That's how come Cody could afford him."

Jeet said nothing.

"A really nice mover, too. You should see—" I squinted. "Jeet," I said, interrupting myself, "you can pour it now. The pot will shut itself off while you . . . " But his look of incomprehension was so complete that I ended up taking the mug away from him and demonstrating.

A thick stream of Starbuck's Christmas blend scented the room, or maybe even the house.

"See?" I went on. "It has this little shutoff thing, so you can pull it out while it's still brewing." A marvel I never ceased to applaud, impatient type that I am.

I handed him the cup, and, hot as it was, he took a sip. It seemed to shiver through his body. Finally he was able to speak. "I don't think it should be making all that noise," he said.

"What? The pot?"

"Yes, the pot."

"Oh."

Because I'd hit the switch and headed outside, I had no idea whether it usually made all that racket or not. But anyway, the coffee was wonderful. "Did you hear what I said? About Lola's new horse?"

"What horse?" Jeet asked.

So I had, in effect, been talking to the wall.

"Cody bought her a horse for Christmas. A beautiful horse. Except he charges and Lola has to rehabilitate him."

Jeet said something like "Hmmph," and continued sipping.

"I didn't get to see him do it," I said. "Charge, I mean. So probably Lola hasn't put him in a situation that would get him going." Except that she did tell me he would, so maybe she had. And maybe that was why she had him in one of the few stalls she had that didn't have a run.

I hadn't thought to ask.

Jeet was on his feet now, yawning, stretching. He

slipped into tattered fleece-lined slippers—I'd planned to get him new ones for Christmas, but I hadn't gone searching for them yet; I mean, I still had six days, right?—grabbed the as yet unfurled newspaper, and headed toward the bathroom.

"Did you hear a word I said?" I called after him. "About Lola's horse?"

About half an hour later, as I stood outside filling the water trough, I asked the question again.

Jeet, on his way to work, had paused at the paddock to say good-bye. Looking at him, crisp in khaki trousers and a V-neck sweater, a bright white oxford cloth collar and cuffs showing beneath it, you would never guess the stupor he'd been in earlier.

I squinted at the shirt. Bright white with purple stripes.

"I heard you," Jeet said. "What did he use? American Express?" Jeet laughed, as though it was a great joke.

"Huh?" I said.

"Who ever heard of charging a horse," he explained.

"I don't know what you're talking about," I said, turning the faucet off in case I hadn't heard him correctly.

I looked down at his feet. At his beige socks, to be exact.

"The difference between men and women," I said, "is that a woman would wear purple socks to match the stripes in that shirt."

"Oh, yeah?"

"Yeah."

"Well, that's not the difference," he said. "The difference is that men don't *have* purple socks."

I stood and pondered this, and the truth of it was plain as day.

"I've got to run," Jeet said, leaning down and brushing my forehead with his lips. He was carrying one of those thermos cups you can drink out of, the kind with the slit lid. He didn't put his arms around me, therefore, but instead held his arm straight out, so as not to spill any of the brew.

Coffee, I should tell you, is about the only thing I can make that tastes okay. In fact, I make great coffee, Jeet says, and he is, after all, a gourmet. I mean, in addition to the book he's writing about food, he is the food editor at the *Austin Daily Progress*. He used to just review restaurants, and he still does from time to time, but not that often since he got his promotion.

Actually I miss the restaurant thing, because we got to eat very fancily on the paper's nickel. Now we hardly ever go out because we can't much afford it. Plus, once Jeet gets home, he doesn't feel like going back into Austin, whereas, when reviewing was his job, I'd often meet him downtown and we'd gorge.

I can't think of anything neater than gorging and being paid for it. But I digress.

"Would you like Santa to bring you purple socks?" I asked.

The look on his face served as a reply—the kind of look that Cary Grant used to get in those wonderful old comedies of his. The kind that combined, *Is she for real?* with *Have I come to the right planet?*

"Don't forget to pick up butter," I said, returning to the prosaic. Tomorrow was a Saturday, and usually on Saturdays, Lola and Cody wandered over to see what was cooking.

Jeet had mentioned something about homemade

tortillas and ghee. Even I knew you couldn't make ghee without butter.

"Oh, bad news, hon," Jeet said.

"What?"

"I have to be in El Paso."

"El Paso?"

"A cookie bake," he said.

"When do you leave?"

"Early," he said.

"You mean tomorrow?"

"Yup. Seven something."

"You leave here at seven something?"

"No," he corrected me. "Worse. The *plane* leaves at seven something."

"Oh, God."

"Don't worry about it. You don't have to get up. I'll just creep off into the night."

"Oh, right." I was envisioning one of Jeet's last-minute searches for whatever: his car keys, his plane ticket, his camera. "How long will you be gone?"

"Depends. There might be a chili thing the day after, and, if there is, I might as well stay for it."

"A chili thing," I whined. "But it's practically Christmas."

"You're right," he said. "Maybe it's tamales. I'll bet it is. I'll bet it's tamales."

Tamales are a Mexican staple at Christmastime, with whole families getting together for days and days in order to make them. Us gringos order them by the dozens, and nowadays, you can get vegetarian ones, too.

"Bring some home," I said. Small consolation.

* * *

When Saturday morning came, the pounding at the door made me realize that I hadn't bothered informing Cody and Lo that we would be gheeless. What was worse, I sat up and was almost knocked back down by a fierce, pounding headache.

Cedar Fever.

How else could I have slept through my usual horse-feeding time?

I know it sounds like a made-up disease, but here in Texas, and especially near Austin, where all the allergens come to party, Cedar Fever is a very real thing. It makes you feel flulike, in that ache-all-over way. And you get the other symptoms, too: the runny nose, the burning eyes, sore throat, et cetera. It happens around Christmastime, too, when cedar blooms and releases its pollen into the atmosphere.

It sounds like a perfect start for a science-fiction story, but really, even weathercasters give the cedar-pollen count along with the temperature here.

We'd pretty much cleared our property of cedar, but it grew rampant wherever land was untended. Which is lots of places all around us. Which, usually, we thought of as a plus.

Me, I'd occasionally get hit with it. Like now.

I staggered downstairs and found myself face-to-face with Cody.

I groaned.

"Thanks," he said. "Same to you."

"No, really," I told him. "I just have Cedar Fever is all."

He watched me stagger around and realized that I was telling him the truth. "Here," he said, reaching back into his jean pocket. "I've got just the thing."

I watched as he pulled a narrow paper package

out. It was filled with white powder. "Give me some water," he demanded.

I filled a glass and watched him.

"Is this legal?" I asked.

He laughed. "Very," he said. "It's a headache powder." He poured it into the glass and swished the water around until the powder dissolved. "Drink this," he said, handing it to me.

"I don't know," I said.

"Drink it," he ordered. "And by the time you've fed your horses, you'll be A-OK."

I drank it, figuring Cody wasn't about to poison me, but not really trusting the stuff to work. And yet, as I moved around filling scoops and running water and pitching the hay, the cloud of pain that had initially enveloped me began to dispel.

And sure enough, by the time I came back into the kitchen, I was feeling the way I usually felt: great.

"What was that again?" I asked him.

He pulled a little blue-and-white envelope out of his pocket and handed it to me. "B. C. headache powder," he said. "My mama's sweet old-fashioned remedy for Cedar Fever, colds, and what-have-you."

"And you get it where?"

"In the drugstore. At the H.E.B. 'Wherever fine headache products are sold.' Here," he said, handing me the envelope. "Take these. I'm probably not going to need them."

"Just give me a couple," I said, putting two of the little packets on the table and giving him back the rest. They were odd little things, though. Translucent paper around a fine white powder. "They look like heroin or something," I said.

"As if you know what heroin looks like."

"I've seen movies," I said. "So where's Lola?"

"Still back at the ranch. Where's Jeet?"

"El Paso. But hey, that won't stop us."

Jeet had brought home a beautiful loaf of sourdough bread yesterday. No kidding. I'd been eyeing the shiny and even thumpable crust of the loaf since he'd brought it home, but I'd restrained myself by visualizing my already pudgy body in riding breeches.

I mean, there I'd be, ballooning out over the saddle while all of these sylphs, Lola among them, rode past.

Jeez. If I gave into my food-loving instincts, I'd be barred from the show ring for aesthetic reasons.

Which reminds me, I'd just seen an ad for plus-size riding clothes.

Plus-size riding clothes.

I didn't need them yet, but it was good to know they were out there. It was only a matter of time.

Maybe I would tear the ad out of the magazine.

"Stop us from what?" Cody said.

"Eating," I answered. "But why didn't Lo come with you?"

"She's messing with the horse," Cody said. "What did you think of him?"

"He was great," I said. "So where'd you get him?"

"The price of that info is a stack of tortillas," Cody said. "So what are we going to eat? I've been thinking about Jeet's tortillas all morning."

I smiled. Who'd have thought that Cody and I would find such a large common ground? "I've got his tortilla recipe."

Of course, as I told you, the minute I saw that loaf of bread, I'd planned to make sourdough toast. But now that the word *tortilla* had been uttered, I'd have killed for one.

Even the store-bought ones are good.

But Jeet's tortillas, ah . . .

I moved toward the little room that Jeet used as his office. Sure enough, I found the box with his manuscript.

Remember I mentioned his book? Well, it's a memoir about all of the food he'd grown up with, recipes and euphoric recollections.

I flipped through the pages and there it was: a sheet labeled *Carmen's Tortillas.*

Cody seemed to have heard about my culinary skills, because as I was searching out a bowl, he was protesting, "No, hey. Toast or something—dry cereal, maybe—will be fine."

I ignored him, naturally, babbling—as I assembled the ingredients—about how Jeet's recipes were from people he knew when he was little, neighbors and relatives and such, and how I had no idea who Carmen was, blah, blah, blah.

Which was just as well.

Because inside minutes, I wanted to totally mutilate Carmen.

Maybe it was because I didn't know where Jeet kept his rolling pin. Maybe that was it. Because failing to find it meant I needed to substitute something with which I could roll out portions of the dough.

But hey, I was imaginative. I figured I'd use a drinking glass.

Well.

I think I have to tell Jeet to amend his recipe—or at least attach a warning—because Carmen's tortillas, given half a chance, will affix themselves to any surface they contact.

Or maybe I should use the singular, *tortilla*, because at this point, the stuff was one immense oozy white lump.

And Cody was protesting by now that he actually wasn't hungry.

"It's too late." I glowered at him, reaching for a second drinking glass. "And besides, I know what I forgot."

The flour. I dredged the glass in flour, because I thought I'd seen Jeet do that—or something like it—and I tried to roll again.

It made no difference. The second glass ended up all coated with tortilla dough.

"Robin, really." Cody was pacing around now, and gesturing wildly with his arms. "Coffee's actually enough for me. Uh . . . "

But, with a gleam in my eye, I took a dishtowel and wrapped it around yet a third drinking glass. "No, it's fine," I assured my guest. "I think I've seen my grandmother do this."

Actually it wasn't my own grandmother. It was Lucy Gomez's grandmother, but, for Cody's peace of mind, I didn't want to distance myself too far from the expertise. Anyway, this was going to work.

Except that now, Carmen's tortilla dough was all over the towel and my hands—and my shirt, and the counter, and the cutting board, and the sink, and the cabinets beneath the sink.

"I've got to get out of here," Cody said. "No kidding, Robin. I'm really starting to worry about Lola."

I looked up from the mess. "What do you mean?" I asked him.

"I've been here half an hour. She was coming right behind me. I'm scared."

I looked down at what had been a mountain of dough. There was barely enough left for one tortilla. The rest of it was coated all over every surface in the room. "You're just saying that," I accused him.

"No," he said. "This horse comes at you like gangbusters."

"So what?" I said. "Lo knows how to deal with that."

"I mean it," Cody said, walking toward the door. The somber look on his face said more than his words.

"Did you walk over?" I asked him.

"Yes."

"Well, come on. I'll drive."

And I led the way to Mother—that's my truck—sticky hands and sticky clothes and all.

"Cody"—I was turning Mother around when I finally had the courage to ask—"what's the story here?"

"The horse ran right over his last owner," he said. "Literally." He took a deep sigh. "And she's dead."

CHAPTER 3

"I can't believe this," I said, as I swerved onto the shoulder of the road and then back on again. "You actually bought a killer horse for the woman you allegedly love?"

"Oh, give me a break," Cody said. "The horse is a rehab. He charges, yes—and his last owner *did* come to grief—but Lola knows all about it. She said it was no big deal. She could fix it, she said."

"Did you actually see what the horse did?" I demanded.

"The, uh . . . widower had a video," he told me, "so, yes."

"And did Lola see this video?"

"I don't know," he admitted. "I brought it home with me, but I don't know if she ever watched it."

We were turning into LoCo's driveway now. I asked, "How bad was it?"

"Hurry up, okay?"

We—by which I mean anybody driving onto the place—usually drove very slowly up Lola's driveway, because the otherwise devil-may-care Lola seemed convinced that her three cats were lurking along the way, just waiting for an opportunity to hurl themselves under our churning wheels.

Today, however, we all but barreled up at a cat-killing pace.

As I braked, I couldn't resist saying, "How could you?" to my distraught passenger.

But there, on the horizon, was Lola, mounted on her Christmas gift. She glanced over and waved. Cody and I waved back and then both exhaled a deeply felt sigh of relief.

Now it was Cody's turn. "You should talk," he said. "Horses are big animals. They hurt people sometimes."

He was talking about my own Spier, I knew. "That was an accident," I said. "You sound as though this horse aims first."

"I'll show you the video," he said. "You'll see. The former owner just about trained him to do it."

"Oh, right," I said sarcastically. "Is that how come you could afford him?" I asked.

"You got it," he said.

Lola, obviously thrilled with her new horse, dispelled the combative mood that by this time Cody and I were in. She came riding up, all smiles. The horse, who'd grown a winter coat, was sweating in the December heat. I laid a hand on his damp chest, out of habit.

"I'll walk him out," Lola responded. "But I want to show you something first." She turned toward the area we used as an arena, and Cody and I walked behind her.

I don't know what Cody was thinking, but I looked at that horse's rear end and saw power.

"I thought he was just green-broke," Lola said, breaking into a trot, "but look."

We watched her come down the long side in shoulder-in.

"And that's not all," Lola called, coming down the center line at a canter this time, and then doing a half-pass back to the wall.

"Whew," I said appreciatively.

Lo let the reins go lax; the horse's neck went stretching down. Lo patted him, telling us, "He's had some really good training."

I looked at Cody quizzically. "Not from his last owner," he said. "She was a ding-a-ling. Did you watch that tape, Lo?" he asked.

"Uh-uh, not yet. I will, though."

You'd better, I thought.

As if countering my objection, Lola added, "I haven't put him in a situation where he *could* charge yet."

"Good thinking," Cody said.

Lo plopped onto the ground and began running the stirrups up. Then she took the reins over the horse's head and led him back toward the barn. "How's this?" she asked. "I'll turn him out in that paddock over there"—she pointed at a grassy enclosure about twice the size of the run—"and then, while all three of us are here, I'll go in there, get him, and lead him back to the barn."

"Okay," Cody and I chorused.

Lola's voice grew thick in her throat. "Cody," she said, "he's the best horse I've ever owned. I'm going to call him Noel. You know, for Christmas."

"I'll fill that trough out there," I announced, feeling that I was intruding on what was a private moment.

But then Lola looked at me and said, "You might want to rinse yourself off before you go inside,

Robin. I don't know what it is, but there's some kind of white guck all over you."

I had a brief flash of Jeet waking up and wandering into our dough-laden kitchen, but then I remembered he was gone. He was probably, right this very minute, weighing the aesthetic effect of toasted as opposed to virgin coconut or some such.

"In fact, I'll bring you a towel," Lo added.

Cody pointed at me and started laughing. "She tried making tortillas," he said. "You should have seen it. I wish I had *that* on tape."

Lo smiled down at us. "You don't know how good it is," she said, "to see the two of you really getting along."

Cody had gone inside to pop the tape into the VCR. The trough was nearly full when Lo and Noel came out.

She led the horse into the enclosure, then turned him and led him back toward the gate. "I don't want to take any chances," she said. Then she slipped the halter off and stepped back through to the outside.

We watched as Noel went along the fence line, checking his new digs out. He trotted along easily, whinnying at the horses in the farther field.

We laughed as they whinnied back, their voices varying from what we called skinny-whinnies to Noel's own basso profundo.

Then he stopped, folded up his front legs, and began to ease down.

"He's going to roll," Lola said, amused.

I don't know why, but it's always fun to watch horses roll. Usually they do it in mud or after they've been ridden. I always imagine that they're trying to divest themselves of human stink.

But the thing was, this horse, Noel, didn't go down all the way. Instead, he hovered in that halfway-to-the-ground position and began to graze.

"Will you look at that?" Lola said, amazed. "I think this boy's been hobbled."

Hobbled is an old-fashioned way of confining a horse by tying his front legs together. It's cheaper than fences and it does keep them from galloping off. It was probably done by cowboys out on the open range, but other than that, you don't see it, not here.

Except that I *had* seen it before, at a farm about sixty miles away. I had seen a horse do exactly what this guy, Noel, was doing. It had been a horse who was the very same color, too: brown.

It wasn't anything I wanted to think about, but I couldn't stop the images from rolling once they had begun.

The horse, legs bent just this way, grazing.

And a few hours later, the horse flat on the ground, dead.

What was his name, that horse?

Wickie.

Wickie. Short for Wickingham.

One of Louanne Perry's horses.

It was the reason Noel had looked familiar when I'd first seen him yesterday. Because he was Wickie, the dead horse Wickie resurrected. Oh, God.

"What's the matter with you?" Lola said. "You look as though you've seen a ghost."

I smiled wanly.

I had.

CHAPTER 4

Without meaning to, I segued into a part of the past that I have tried to forget. A part of the past that—until this very moment—I thought I had successfully forgotten. A part of the past that scares me, that has made me turn down numerous requests for help—requests that could bring in extra cash—cash for me, cash I could always use for riding lessons, sweat sheets, hoof dressing, and so on.

Because Wickie—Wickingham—died while he was under my care. I mean while I was horse-sitting.

There, I've said it.

But saying it doesn't provide any measure of relief. If anything, it brings the whole thing back with a super clarity that's like one of those computer-generated sunsets. Too real.

Okay, okay. I'll tell you.

It was about three years ago when I picked up the phone to find Louanne Perry—yes, *the* Louanne Perry, the Perry heiress that everyone in the horse business not only talked about but made fun of—on the phone.

No one had actually met her, mind you. People

had just heard from a friend of a friend, that kind of thing. You know how that goes.

Well, that was pretty much how she'd heard about me, heard that I would fill in for vacationing owners to pick up some extra cash. I would be helping her out tremendously, she said.

I think I said something noncommital, like "Hmm."

And then she said that she had to go away to some retreat—I think the word *self-actualization* was used—and she had no one, absolutely no one, to come in and take care of her horses.

So would I—for a hundred and fifty dollars a day—take care of her six horses? Feed them twice a day and pick up stalls?

In fact, she said, if I wanted to, I could live at her house while I was doing it. It was just three days. In fact, she'd like that because she hated to leave the place vacant . . . and everyone had quit on her.

She began enumerating the staff members who'd walked out. The trainer and the stable boys (plural), and the maids (plural again) and her driver.

But she absolutely could not cancel her self-actualization retreat. I don't remember why. Probably her identity would be lost forever without it.

But I'm being snide.

Still, everything in me was saying no, no way, no thank you. I mean, wasn't it a bad sign that everyone had quit? And besides, I'd only sat for people I knew, people who lived near me so that I could drive there and drive back home. This was sixty miles away. I didn't know anybody who had ever been there, either.

"Please," she asked. And she sounded so sweet, so sincere, so desperate. "Two hundred a day," she tried. The going rate was something like twenty-five dollars! I'm talking max!

"No," I said. "Plus that's way too much." She was going to get some greedy fortune hunter or something in there if she wasn't careful.

Then she said that I could bring my own horse—or even a couple of horses—with me.

I could use her indoor arena to ride in.

I could use her indoor pool to swim in. Her little gymnasium to work out in. Her Jacuzzi to loll in . . .

Well, you get the picture.

This was like Club Med—only in this case, I wouldn't be paying, I'd be getting paid. It was like, pinch yourself already.

Oh, and this one horse, Wickie, had been trained to Fourth Level, and, if I wanted to, I could ride him, too. She had just gotten him, she said, and hadn't really had a chance to ride him herself.

Oy. Talk about temptation!

And this offer came when Jeet was off on some food trip—I think a morel mushroom expedition in the Blue Ridge Mountains or something. He was writing about how to find these mushrooms and compiling old-timers' recipes about using them. I mean, he couldn't even be reached by phone all that week.

And a hundred and fifty dollars a day! That would mean I could pay for some extra riding lessons. Lots of riding lessons with that much cash. Because I wasn't going to take two-hundred dollars. The heavens would open and I'd be struck dead if I did that.

Yes, I said, ignoring my instincts.

Well, it was a nightmare.

There were six horses.

Wickie.

Wackie, who was named after the town of Waxahachie.

And no, not Woo, but Willie, whose real name was Wilshire, as in Boulevard.

I don't remember what the other ones were called.

Wickie, the Fourth Level horse, was brown. And Wickie, who'd been trained in Panama, had been hobbled. He always folded his front legs as if about to roll in order to eat and to drink. Louanne showed me this, saying she was hoping she could train him to do it on command, so that it would look as though he was taking a bow.

Except that Louanne couldn't have trained ivy up a wall.

Louanne was extremely tentative around her horses, and you could see that it was only a matter of time before they'd figure it out and take advantage of her.

Horses are opportunists in that way.

And they aren't dogs. They're big, and, albeit that it's usually inadvertent, they can hurt you.

But that's pretty much beside the point.

To the point is why it was that all of Louanne's help had abandoned her.

The reason was Louanne herself. She was fussiness personified.

And fussiness with no rhyme or reason behind it.

She seemed, vis-à-vis the horses, to have acquired all of her knowledge via some kiddie horse program on TV, the kind where you whistle and the horse, out on the prairie, hears you and comes to your rescue or something. Because that was her approach. At variance, shall we say, with reality.

I know, I sound like a creep talking about Louanne Perry this way, but she was a joke.

She told me, for instance, that I had to keep an eye on all the water buckets in case a horse should contaminate the bucket with a shaving, say, or a strand of hay.

Contaminate, yes.

In which case, I shouldn't just fish out said contaminant.

No.

I had to pour out the water and rinse the pail and refill it.

I was to patrol the barn hourly, in fact—like the rest rooms at Howard Johnson or something—and do that.

So you can imagine how Louanne was about poops.

I mean, she practically expected me to be standing there with a net to catch them in midair.

Which, of course, given that there were six horses, would have been impossible.

So I was on continual poop patrol, too.

She said that she wished there were someone to spell me during the night, when I might be sleeping, because she hated to think of her babies in their stalls with an eight-hour accumulation of poops.

Her babies.

And then she looked at me longingly, as though I should voluntarily renounce sleep.

I know you must think I'm exaggerating, but really, I'm not.

And it got worse.

Each horse had a sheet and two blankets—a lightweight and a polar weight one—and, if the temperature in the barn fell below seventy, I was to put the sheet on.

If it fell below fifty, it was blanket time.

She had never had to use the polar weights, she admitted, but they were there nonetheless, just in case.

And it wasn't as though these horses had been clipped or anything.

I mean, we're talking Austin, Texas, here. Not Buffalo, New York, or Duluth, Minnesota. Not Siberia.

The three days loomed before me like the Gobi Desert. Four days would have killed me.

But that isn't all.

Louanne believed that the horses would miss her.

Rather than have them fretting, she had made each of them two audiotapes. One for morning. One for beddie-bye. Her word, not mine. I was to stand at the stall doors and play said tapes.

I asked her how long she'd been around horses.

She said, predictably, about six months.

I said something about a horse management course.

She said her vet—a man I'd never heard of named Ornell Standish—had given her one.

He was the man who had gotten her into horses.

I would meet him if I took the job because he had to interview me, too.

Well, maybe he'll hate me, I thought hopefully. I mean, some people do. Or maybe he'll mention to Louanne that seven-eighths of the tasks she wanted done were stupid and unnecessary. "Bogus," I guess, is the current term. "Out to lunch" is the old-fashioned one.

Sure, I thought, bring the man on. Bring the man

on before I have to stand in front of stalls with crazy audiotapes blaring Louanne's voice. Before my hands chap from swishing out water buckets and clasping and unclasping blankets.

I mean, she had to be exaggerating about him having taught her. And even if he had, hadn't she ever picked up a stable management book? Couldn't she see that there were maybe easier ways?

Or had her fortune influenced him? Had it—the thought of all those pots of money—led him to allow poor Louanne to carry on with all her silly notions about how horses ought to be cared for, completely obliterating their horse-ness, as it were?

I mean, if Louanne could have kept the animals in little velvet-lined jewelry cases (and yes, it makes me think of coffins, too), she would have. And Ornell Standish—a vet whose word the woman probably would have heeded—let her be that way.

Why?

He was either a jerk or a liar.

Jerk, I think I decided, because he cruised onto Louanne's property in a little bitty sports car. I mean, what vet, and here in Texas, too, doesn't drive a pickup truck?

And he gets out and he's wearing a suit! A whiteish suit. And he's wearing a big, expensive-looking watch and a pinkie ring.

It wasn't just what he was wearing, though, it was the way he looked. Sort of too big for his clothes, as though he'd refused to admit that he'd gained weight—and so there he was, straining every seam, his cuffs hiked up too short by the expanse of his belly, his eyes bulging due to the too-tight collar of his shirt.

So I couldn't tell if he was too pink—his skin tone, I mean—naturally or because he was slowly being strangled.

His face was round and jowly and covered with the sheen of sweat. His smile was too broad and his eyes were too bright. And he was out of breath, just from the effort of getting out of the low-slung car and walking toward us.

"Isn't he an angel?" Louanne whispered.

Right. That was exactly it. He looked like a cherub gone bad. An oversized cherub at that.

But still, he was the person I hoped would bring Louanne to her senses, right?

Then Louanne immediately started boasting about how she'd followed his instructions to the letter and how happy the horses were as a result.

I made some really understated comment about nature, here—I don't remember exactly what—and he ignored me.

I mean, he flat out ignored me.

And worse, he just kept on doting on Louanne, laughing way too heartily at her insipid little insights and acting as though she should be out lecturing at vet schools on stable care.

Like when Louanne was yammering about this business of the water—you know, never letting a strand of hay rest in the water to contaminate it, and changing the water three hundred times as a result—instead of saying, *Louanne, that really isn't necessary*, he actually told her she was doing great! No little wink at me to indicate he thought Louanne ought to have some sense shaken into her. Nothing!

Never mind that I was the one who was going to be changing all that water!

And it was the same with the tape recorder thing

I told you about. He congratulated her on it when he ought to—What? Have had the tapioca syphoned from her brain pan!

Oh, I know what you're thinking. That I don't like to be wrong. And you're right, I don't. And here I was, right as rain, and being treated as though I needed to have Louanne Perry give me a crash course in taking care of horses.

I should have said, *Listen, Louanne. You and this vet here both belong in the San Diego Zoo.* Instead, I let the lure of a hundred and fifty dollars per day zip my mouth shut. I actually think I smiled while the two of them were seconding each other about this stuff.

And I know, I know. I came perilously close to mimicking the very behavior that I found so reprehensible in Standish. But he was a vet! I was just an impoverished housewife; he was a professional!

But anyway, Ornell Standish approved of my shuck-and-jive and I got the job.

And the thing is, I felt guilty enough to actually do all that she'd asked me to do, right down to standing at the stall doors playing those stupid tapes!

But none of that really matters now.

What matters is that Wickie, the brown one from Panama who'd been hobbled, the one who was trained to Fourth Level in dressage, died.

It was the second day.

The second day—and there he was, dead.

I saw him as I approached the barn, out at the end of his run. I knew that something was wrong the minute I laid eyes on him, because he was down when he ought to have been standing there in a state of high anticipation.

In fact, he ought to have been standing near the stall door, by the feed bucket.

And he wasn't just down.

He was down with his legs jutting out very stiffly.

I mean, sometimes horses can do that and be very, very still, and you have a little *Oh, no!* twinge, but then they blink, or they groan, or they do something that lets you know everything's okay.

This was a stillness that was absolute.

A stillness that I can't forget.

I opened his stall door and I ran out there, kind of choking as I did so, and I laid a hand on him.

And that was all it took to know that I was right. Yes, he was dead. He was cold and he was, I don't know, unyielding, like an animal who'd been stuffed by a taxidermist or something.

I thought I'd throw up.

Oh, I know. You're thinking, *Hasn't she ever seen an animal dead before?* But the truth is no. Not like that. You don't see dead horses lying on the road the way you do dogs and cats, after all. And the one and only horse I've ever had who did die, did it at the vet's. I mean, that's the way most horses die, either put down when some treatment fails or after a gross injury. The vet comes and they're carted off. You don't see them—oh, yuck—stiffening before your very eyes.

Okay. I'm a real weenie about this kind of thing; you're right.

I ran to the phone, grateful that Ornell Standish's number was plastered there on the tack room wall, and I called, barely able to make myself understood.

And he came right over. He said he'd take care of everything. I wasn't soothed by this.

I was unsoothable. I couldn't even watch when they came up Louanne's long drive with something that looked like a front-end loader to take Wickie's corpse away.

And I couldn't get hold of Jeet—and I didn't want to get hold of Louanne, even if that had been possible.

I called Lola.

And Lola came and waited with me the next day when Louanne came home.

It's got to be the worst time I've ever lived through.

Maybe if Louanne hadn't been so nice about it, I'd have felt better. But she didn't yell, she didn't scream—she didn't chastise me or even mention the word *lawsuit*.

She just patted my arm and looked defeated—and whipped out her checkbook and paid me the four hundred and fifty dollars.

Blood money.

It's probably the only check I've ever gotten that I didn't dash right to the bank with. In fact, I entertained thoughts of never, ever, cashing it. I eventually did, but it took me way longer than it ever had before.

Because of my guilt.

Oh, I know, I know; it really wasn't my fault—but it was my worst fear realized.

And the thing is, Standish said it had been colic, too—so that almost made it my fault, since colic is usually related to feeding errors.

Because that was another thing—the feeding, I mean. Each of those horses got a precise amount of various separate substances, like corn and molasses and—well, actually, every ingredient that's in sweet feed, which makes you wonder why she didn't just feed that. But of course, one horse had whole oats and another crimped, and a third would get rolled, et cetera.

It was stupid.

But I kept wondering if I'd somehow gotten the proportions wrong, although even if I did, I didn't see how that would have brought on a colic, anyway.

And when had it happened?

Not during the day, when I'd have seen and called Standish immediately so that Wickie could have been saved.

No.

It came while I—worn out from a swim and a hot Jacuzzi—had been sleeping.

Sleeping!

Well, of course, Lola said the obvious: that it could have happened with Louanne there just as easily. But it didn't help. And to this day, I will never feed for anyone. I mean anyone except Lola. In Lola's case, I think I'm grateful that she, knowing, would even ask me once in a while.

But maybe you think I'm making too big a thing out of this Wickie episode. I don't know, but the point of it is this: I swear that Lola's gift horse, Noel, isn't Noel at all.

I think the horse is Wickie.

Not Wickie reincarnated, but Wickie himself.

Which, of course, isn't possible.

CHAPTER 5

When I snapped back to the present, Lola and Cody were standing there, looking at me with grave concern.

"You okay?" Lola asked.

"I don't know," I said. "I was thinking about that horse Louanne Perry had. Wickingham."

"Oh, God," Lola said. "You promised you wouldn't."

"But do you remember him?"

"I never saw him," Lola said. "He was, well . . . you know, dead when I even heard about him."

"But did you see him? When he was . . . you know."

"No. That creepy vet had hauled him off. Remember?"

That was right.

"What are you two talking about?" Cody interrupted.

And I decided to drop it.

Because how was I going to tell Lola what I thought? How was I going to tell her in a way that she'd believe? A way that wouldn't make her think that I was crazy?

Except that the hobble thing was just too unusual to be coincidence.

"Look," I said to Lola and Cody, "I have to go back home. Jeet is out of town and I've got to . . . uh . . . clean the kitchen," both of which were true.

"Jeet is out of town?" Lola said.

"Cookie bake," I explained. "Plus there's going to be some tamale thing."

"Well, don't just clean the kitchen." Cody laughed. "Clean yourself up while you're at it."

Lola threw an arm around Cody's waist—and Lola was, I noted, looking especially happy. Probably because, as she'd said earlier, Cody and I really did seem to be hitting it off. Anyway, Cody did the same thing with his arm, and together they walked back toward the house they share. And I had one of those moments, you know the kind, where everything was sort of glowing and warm and exactly the way Christmas is supposed to be.

Except that minutes later, I was driving back to Primrose Farm at a speed of about five miles an hour, thinking all the while about how I was going to figure out if there was any way that Noel could actually *be* Wickie.

But the thing is, if this were a *Columbo* or something, it would work this way: The evil veterinarian would have substituted a dead brown horse for Wickingham, then spirited Wickingham away for . . . resale?

Ha! Like maybe "Wickie" had died quite a number of times. You could make a lot of money selling a Fourth Level horse over and over again.

Except that the dressage community is not that big. You'd get caught. Besides, where would you keep the ringer? And would he really be dead? He'd have to be, I guess. So you'd need, oh, yuck, a meat locker someplace where you'd whip this corpse out . . .

This was getting too gross for me. Also, it seemed impossible. And I had more pressing problems anyway, in the form of my kitchen.

My heart fell when I saw it. Somehow, when Cody and I had left, the urgency had worked to screen the mess I'd made. Now, there it was, and dried, too.

I picked at one of the blobs of dry dough, and, when it flaked, I figured it wouldn't be *too* bad to clean.

At least Jeet wouldn't see it in this condition. There was that to be grateful for.

What would I need to begin? Something like a windshield scraper, maybe. The kind they use up North when their windshields freeze. But where would I get one?

Because I couldn't use anything wet. It would just make the dough all dribbly—and then it would dry again, thinner, but over a wider area.

Oy.

I decided to make a phone call first.

I was barely able to convince the receptionist at the vet clinic that I didn't have to have a sick or dying animal to want to talk to Dr. Reasoner.

Then I listened to a very tinny version of "Silver Bells" while I waited for him to come on.

When he did, I asked, "Len, do you remember that creepy vet who used to live someplace north of here? Ornell Standish?"

Len sighed. I knew he was going to go into his shtick about how I ought to preface any questions with a long, hi-how-are-you thing, but then thought better of it. Instead he said, "Oh, Robin."

"What?"

"Why can't you keep yourself out of trouble?"

"What do you mean?"

"I mean, why can't you let well enough alone? Why do you have to be messing around where you shouldn't ought to be all of the time? Why—?"

"What? Do you know something about Standish? Something sinister?" I asked, interrupting.

"I only know that I didn't like the man. And that I was glad when he pulled up stakes."

"To go where?" I persisted.

"How in tarnation am I supposed to know? Do you think that I go around asking a lot of rude questions? I tell you, girl, if you don't—"

I barged in on his flow of words again. "How would I find out? Where he is, I mean."

"Damned if I know. It's Saturday, and Monday it'll be . . . what? Just a couple of days before Christmas—and probably any of the veterinary registries that would know will be closed, or else not up to doing a lot of research. Especially for someone who doesn't know how to say 'please,' and 'thank you.' "

"I always say 'please,' " I said. "And I think that I usually say 'thank you,' too." I mean, I was pretty sure.

Len sighed again, resignedly this time. "Two things," he said, "and you are not to repeat the first one to anyone, you understand?"

"Yes."

"Number one, I heard he used to deal in research dogs. Now I don't know that it was true, mind you, and I really didn't think he was doing any kind of research of his own, but that was what I heard a long while back. It could just be that the other vets didn't like him, either, and stories like that sometimes get spread around. Usually starts with someone saying 'He's the type who would blah, blah, blah,' and then the next thing you know, people have him doing it."

"And number two?"

"Number two is that I heard he was out in Los Angeles, taking care of movie stars' horses."

Los Angeles.

"Len," I said, "do you believe he was . . . you know—doing research on dogs?" He did have the look of a vivisectionist, if I remembered him correctly.

"Now that's not what I said, missy," Len insisted. Then his voice got lower. "What I heard was that, when he was in vet school, he used to steal dogs and sell them to research labs. Now that's the honest-to-God truth about what I heard. That doesn't mean it was true—and that doesn't mean that I believe it was true. It just means that a lot of people believed some bad stuff about him."

"So he was the kind of person who would fake a horse's death in order to resell a horse?"

"Say what?" Len said.

"I mean, he'd substitute a dead horse for a living horse and then sell the living horse, pretending that the living horse was the dead one."

There was a long silence on the line.

Then Len said, "Are you talking about that business when you were baby-sitting that Louanne Perry's horses?"

"You know about that?" I asked.

"I just know she had one die."

"And who told you that?" I asked, thinking that

I'd like to punch Lola Albright in the nose. Unless, of course, it was Louanne herself who told.

"I'm thinking," Len said. "And frankly, I think it was Ornell Standish who told me at some powwow down at A and M."

"What?" Weren't vets bound by something like the Seal of Confession or something? "What exactly did he say? Like, that I was the reason the horse died?"

"I don't remember," Len said. "I doubt that it was anything that drastic."

"Yeah, I'll bet," I said, unconvinced.

"Can I get back to work now?" Len asked.

Then I tried. "Well, what if the horse really didn't die? What if some other horse died and Standish just made me think it was that horse?"

"Too risky. Too complicated," Len said.

"Why?" I asked.

"It just is. People know their horses. They wouldn't fall for it."

"But what if the people—by which I mean Louanne—were off somewhere."

"Too far-fetched to even think about," he said.

I swallowed, about to tell him about the way the formerly hobbled Wickie would fold up his legs and how Lo's new horse, Noel, did the same thing, when he said he had to go. "But . . . " I said.

"We'll have to talk another time, Robin," he insisted. "I've got the lame, the halt, and the blind to attend to out here."

"But . . . "

"Later," he said, hanging up.

* * *

Except that, even despite what Len had said about risky and complicated, it seemed pretty plausible to me.

But just to be on the safe side, I had to find out what Louanne had meant when she said that Standish got her into horses. Did she mean that he'd sold her the horses? Or what?

And then I had to see if she had pictures of them.

Which would mean going to see her.

Which I kind of dreaded.

I mean, wouldn't you?

But what was the alternative? Stay home and clean the kitchen?

I looked around at it and was out the door in minutes.

CHAPTER 6

I stepped outside and heard a vaguely metallic crash. Also, my toe hurt. I had kicked a large box, apparently delivered by UPS, as I exited. A Christmas present addressed to Jeet and me.

Probably the annual fruitcake from my mother. I always put it out for the birds and they loved it, flying sort of wobbly after indulging.

I read the label.

Nope, it was from Jeet's aunt Edna in Leakey. Pronounced "Lakey" by the natives.

I wrenched it open.

A festive tin was inside.

I pulled the can out and opened it; a heavenly aroma arose and enveloped me.

Shortbread.

Oh, God! Shortbread! Aunt Edna's shortbread, which contains a ton of butter. Oh, yum.

My hand shot toward the interior of the can and I fought the urge mightily, trying to imagine myself riding down the center line of a dressage arena in skintight breeches and a polo shirt.

Did I want rolls of fat to go waving around as I trotted in?

Because that's what shortbread would lead to. Rolls of fat, rippling and jiggling and threatening to gain some seismic force the way suspension bridges do. Seismic force that could get out of control and pull me right off my horse.

No, no, no.

I eased the lid back on and tore off the tag that indicated the shortbread was for Jeet and me. I placed the tin beside me on the front seat of my truck.

No good.

A fantasy started to unspool, my teeth closing down on the shortbread—and tiny, butter-drenched crumbs of it falling to the floor of my mouth.

This was not going to work. I had to get that can somewhere out of my reach.

So I'd give it to Louanne, a wonderful Christmas present.

But meanwhile . . .

I pulled to the side of the road and installed the tin out of harm's way in the expanse of Mother's truck bed.

Which for some reason, reminded me that I had to talk to Cody, too.

So I cruised to Lola's and hollered into the living room, "Cody?"

Nothing.

They must be at the barn.

I walked to the barn and stood in the aisleway and shouted, "Cody?"

Some rustling.

Lola came out of Noel's stall. "I don't know where he went. Probably checking the fence line or something." Then, "What do you want with him anyway?" Her eyes narrowed.

What I wanted, of course, was to ask him the true

skinny about the horse. Like where, exactly, he'd bought the horse and how he'd heard it was for sale, et cetera. And I didn't want Lo to hear.

"What I want," I said, "is to know if this horse has a brother." Which was sort of true. Like a twin brother, maybe.

Lola laughed.

But I thought, hey. Some stallions are extraordinarily prepotent. Maybe the sire of Noel was, too. And maybe if that stallion had covered the very same mare that produced Noel . . .

Well, it was something.

"Okay," Lo said, reentering the stall. "I'll tell Cody you were looking for him. But meanwhile, I want to get Noel's mane pulled."

"Why?"

"I don't know why," she said, with some irritation. "I just want my horses to look especially spiffy at Christmastime."

God. How long it had been since I'd pulled a mane or done even more than a cursory grooming? "Well," I said teasingly, the way people do when they see someone washing their car, "when you're done with him . . . "

So it was off to Louanne's. Where I hadn't been since the day I'd had to tell her about the terrible death of Wickingham.

All the way over there, the thought of seeing her pretty much overpowered the lure of Aunt Edna's shortbread. That, in and of itself, should tell you how lump-in-the-throat I was feeling about seeing her face-to-face.

True, she'd been gracious when the tragedy took

place. But that didn't mean that, given three years to stew about it, she didn't hate my guts.

In which case, I decided, I'd abort my questioning and leave.

It occurred to me—and I'm ashamed to admit it, for the very first time—that I hadn't heard a thing about Louanne in all that three-year period. Which you might think is very unusual. Except that it wasn't, really.

I mean, Louanne lived far enough away so that no one encountered her very much. And she didn't—hadn't ever, as far as I knew—show or take clinics. Basically, all we'd heard about her when she'd first acquired all of her horses, Wickie included, was that she had aquired them. That and the fact that she was a know-nothing. When she'd called me out of the blue to horse-sit, it had been a networking kind of connection, she'd said, which was believable enough.

So, okay. Louanne had dropped off the dressage planet, so to speak.

The dressage community here is pretty small, and everyone is always gossiping about everyone else. In fact, that was one of the things I feared, that Louanne would tell everyone I'd killed her horse.

Oh, I know that sounds like an exaggeration, but it isn't that much of one. And all it would take would be for her to say something to her blacksmith.

Blacksmiths are like the Internet.

Pretty soon, people would be thinking I'd wiped out Louanne's entire stable.

But not a word was said. No one looked at me funny. No one attempted to shield their horses from me when I walked into a barn or onto the show grounds anywhere.

Louanne had kept her mouth shut, for which I was grateful.

Because like everyone, I'd seen some bad things happen in the gossip department.

If you doubt me, try taking a horse on trial. If you decide not to buy said horse, the first thing the owner will say is how run down he is, absolute skin and bones. Then how his training has regressed. Then how his value has dropped because of you. Et cetera.

And the next thing you know, you're a full-blown spoiler of horses.

Leasing a horse is another area where this happens. Everything is fine while you're leasing, but try and quit. You've ruined the horse. Absolutely run him into the ground.

No kidding, I know people this has happened to, and sometimes the aura that surrounds a circumstance like that doesn't go away.

But I digress. Or else I'm reliving the way I felt about the Wickie thing. But does it really matter if a thing is real or if you only think it? I mean, if it's driving you crazy, does it really make a difference?

But Louanne hadn't been out bad-mouthing me, I reminded myself. Ornell Standish was the one who had been doing that. Well, maybe not bad-mouthing, but he had told Len. Probably every time he told someone, my culpability grew, too.

And to think that all this time, I hadn't known it!

Anyway, reminding myself about how mum Louanne herself had been put me in a better frame of mind about the looming confrontation. I mean, I had more or less diluted the dread I felt.

* * *

Imagine my shock when I drove up Louanne's driveway and discovered an empty field where the indoor arena had stood!

And it hadn't recently departed, either. There was grass growing over the expanse. It didn't look like new grass.

So instead of going up to the house, I walked over there, kind of marveling and toeing around in it.

I mean, sometimes you see places where houses have burned down. Places where there are stairs leading up to nothing, or chimneys in the middle of nowhere, and that's always kind of a shock.

This, though . . .

Because indoors are huge—they have to be to accommodate a dressage arena, which is twenty-by-forty meters, minimum, a meter being about a yard. So figure sixty-six feet by twice that. And most indoors, I guess on the theory that if you're putting in a bunch of money, why not a bunch more, are big enough to accommodate the large arena, which is twenty-by-sixty meters.

Pace it out and you'll see that this is a pretty good size.

And in Louanne's case, the arena had six stalls down one long side. They, natch, were gone, too.

I was trying to find at least an outline where the building had stood, but no.

But soon I became aware of several small dogs who had arrived to help me out. Not Chihuahuas, fortunately. You maybe know how I am about those. These were Jack Russell Terriers, which, hitherto, I'd only seen in movies like *The Mask* and on the cover of *Newsweek* and such. Oh, maybe I'd glimpsed a couple of them at horse shows and stuff, but I'd never seen one up close and personal, so to speak.

Anyway, these little dogs, squat little spotted things with their ears charmingly drooping at the tips, were out there sniffing around, as if trying to discern my purpose in being there. There wasn't any barking, any threatening behavior. It was all, kind of, *Hi, can we help?*

Except for one. This one had a ball—and he kept dropping it at my feet, trying to get me to throw it.

I was about to when Louanne's voice said, "Don't. Don't throw it or he'll bother you forever."

I turned . . . and there she was.

"Robin," she said. She seemed genuinely glad to see me. "Merry Christmas."

Which nudged my memory. "Oh," I said, "I've got something for you." I walked past her to the truck and boosted myself into the bed. Then I leaped down, tin in hand. "You'll love these," I said. "Shortbread."

She looked surprised. Then she smiled at me, tears welling in her eyes. She was touched by the gift, which made me feel more than a little guilty.

The dog with the ball kept tossing the thing, grabbing it in his jaws and then letting go as he whipped his head to one side.

It was cute, and I said so.

"He's one of my pups," she said. "He's six months old. I'm doing dogs now," she said, as if to explain the absence of her indoor arena and stables. "He's pet quality, not show, because he doesn't have enough white. They're supposed to be mostly white. In fact . . . " She paused, looking at me hard and biting down on her lower lip as though thinking hard. "Do you have a dog?"

I shook my head no.

Jeet and I had talked about a dog, but it had been a long time ago. When we'd first started seeing each other, in fact. An old dog of mine—she was fifteen—had just died. I'd told Jeet—and I'd meant it then—that I didn't want another one. Plus we were still in school at the time.

Louanne leaned down and scooped the puppy up, ball and all. "Here," she said. "Merry Christmas."

I was about to demur when the puppy dropped the ball and licked my hand as if to say he approved of the transaction.

I laughed. I guess that meant that I approved of it, too. "Well, uh . . . I . . . uh, thank you," I said.

I'd planned to get Jeet those slippers, and I'd added purple socks to my list. I'd even considered a cashmere sweater that I saw at Second Looks. But Christmas was now only five days off and I hadn't done it yet. So I'd give him this dog, I thought. Why not?

"What's his name?" I said, impressed by the intent way that the puppy was staring at me. I mean, what? Did I smell like liver or something? Because he was absolutely riveted on me.

"Officially, he's The Macaroon. I call him 'Rooney,' " she said.

"The Macaroo—ooon." I found myself baby talking. "The Macarooo-oon." Then, "I . . . uh . . . Will he be okay in my truck?"

"Mother!" Louanne said, looking over at it. "I can't believe you still have that thing."

Believe, I thought. She probably had one of those

new Dodge numbers with the Cummins diesel engine in it. That was the truck I lusted after.

Or else, being into dogs and no longer into horses, she didn't have a truck at all.

It made me think of Standish in his little sports car again, and my stomach churned.

"When did all of this get taken down?" I asked, gesturing at the old arena site.

Louanne shrugged. "After Wickie," she said, lowering her eyes. "I just didn't want to, you know, mess around with horses anymore. I mean, after that, people started telling me colic stories and I realized that horses die all the time . . . and I got more and more scared about it."

"I'm sorry." I stepped forward and laid a hand on her arm. I felt so awful. And even though she was some multimillionaire heiress, she was also just a person. A vulnerable person. Vulnerable, especially, to someone like Standish.

"It's okay. I like the dogs a lot better. They're easier to take care of, and if I go out of town, I can kennel them. But the best thing is, I don't have to ride them."

I tried to remember if I'd ever seen her ride, and then I remembered, yes, she'd shown me a video. She'd had, not a seat, but a sort of perch. The kind of posture that'll get you dumped in a hurry. And I remember that the horse she was riding kind of looked at something—not actually shied—and she'd squealed so that I heard it even on the tape.

So maybe the switch was a blessing, rather than something I had to rue.

I took a deep, nerve-gathering breath. "Horses," I said, "are the reason I'm here."

With that I began questioning her about Wickie.

Where she'd bought him was the first thing I wanted to know.

"They all came from Boots LaRue," she said.

Boots LaRue.

He was a legend in the horse biz, a man who'd been dealing, mostly in hunters and jumpers, for years.

He allegedly had a great eye, the kind that could pull the one horse out of a field of thirty with the stuff to go all the way to the top.

I'd read interviews with him, and he was full of stories about how he'd bought this one for five hundred dollars and ended up selling him for a quarter mil. And no one challenged these stories, either.

But as with any horse dealer, there were lots of derogatory stories, too. These—if I remembered the interview correctly—he chalked up to sour grapes, and I believed it.

He was the real thing.

But how had someone like Louanne hooked up with him?

"Oh," she said, "it wasn't me. It was my vet. You remember, Dr. Standish. He arranged for all my horses through LaRue—and he ended up selling them back to him for me, too."

"Do you remember what you paid for Wickie?" I asked. I could almost imagine my own vet, Len, wincing as I asked a question that direct. But hey, she didn't have to answer.

"Oh, I don't know. I could look at my records. But I think Wickie was in the fifty-thousand-dollar range."

I gulped. This is what someone who'd been riding six months needs, right? Standish should be hauled in front of a firing squad, I thought. "Was he insured?" I asked.

"Well . . . he was, yes." She looked troubled.

"What's wrong?" I asked her.

"You don't think I did anything bad, do you? You know, like those big-name riders they're saying killed—"

"No, no, no." I interrupted her. I didn't want to hear about any of that again. It made me so incredibly sad to even think about people hurting horses for money. "No, no."

She smiled her gratitude.

"Do you remember anything about Wickie?" I persisted. "Like his background?"

"Well, he did that hobble thing," she said. "He came from Mexico or Panama or something."

But Boots LaRue was known for his Latin American connections. I remembered that from some of the pieces I'd read, too.

"Do you have a picture of Wickie?" I asked.

"Why?"

I thought fast. "I found a horse that I think looks a lot like him. I thought maybe I could buy him for you. You know, to sort of make up for . . . well. . . ."

Great. What if she said that was terrific? The gesture she was waiting for? I mean, sometimes I can't believe what comes out of my mouth!

"Oh, Robin," she said, duplicating the hand-on-the-forearm gesture of sympathy. "It wasn't your fault. No matter what Dr. Standish said, I really don't hold you respon—"

"What? What did he say?"

"It's water under the bridge," Louanne insisted, kind of clamping her lips together.

I didn't want to fight with her. I just wanted a

chance to hoist Ornell Standish on his own petard. And to do that, step one, I thought, I had to have a picture.

I hung my head. I said, "If you have even a blurry picture of Wickie, I'd like to have it. You know. Something to remember him by."

She looked at me hard; I thought maybe I'd pushed it a little too far. "I'm not sure that's wise," she said.

"My, uh . . . psychiatrist thought it would help." I lowered my head as I said this, partly because I was ashamed of myself for using such a ploy. Except that it turned out the gesture was just right.

"You know," she said, "I have a painting of Wickie. You can have it."

And so, flanked by a tussle of terriers, we went to her garage—where she shuffled through what seemed a lot of canvases. She pulled one from the many and shook the dust from it.

Thus it was that I wended my way homeward with a 36-by-48 gilt-framed oil painting and an adorable Jack Russell Terrier puppy in tow.

It could have been a lot worse.

CHAPTER 7

I left the puppy in the truck and walked through the kitchen as if I couldn't see the streaks and clumps of tortilla dough that had dried on every surface. If I turned the puppy—I had to start calling him Rooney, because he wouldn't be a puppy forever—loose in here, would he clean things up? Or would he just smear the dough around, or maybe eat too much and blimp up like a little furry spotted beach ball?

But the thing is, the place was such an incredible mess that I couldn't stand being in it.

And, on the other hand, I couldn't stand the notion of tackling it, either.

Maybe when it dried for a couple of days it would flake right off and all I'd have to do was sweep.

With that fond hope, I got back into Mother and drove over to LoCo Farms. Lola was getting into her Suburban when I pulled up.

"How's the horse?" I asked.

She knew I meant Noel. "The same. With Christmas upon us," she said, "I haven't really done much of anything with him."

She shrugged, and I shrugged back.

"I'm going to the outlet malls in San Marcos," she said. "Wanna go?"

"I need to talk to Cody," I said.

She looked momentarily puzzled. Then she said, "What about?"

"I don't know," I said. "Stuff."

She powered up Piggo's window, rather hurriedly, I thought, announcing from behind it that she'd see me around. Then she drove off.

I turned to watch her as she slowly made her way down the drive, and she kept looking back at me in the rearview mirror.

It was weird. But then, Lola's often in a rotten mood. She's beautiful enough to get away with it, if you know what I mean. If I acted the way she acts, I thought disgustedly, I probably wouldn't even have Jeet.

And did Len Reasoner ever lecture Lola about her behavior? Heck, no.

Cody was in the living room, crumpling newspaper for a fire.

"Think you'll need one?" I asked.

"Probably not," he said, "But I want to be ready just in case."

"Cody," I said, "I want to know about this horse. But also, I need you to keep Jeet's present over here so he doesn't find it."

"Fine," he said. "Where is it?"

"It's in the truck."

"Is it heavy?"

"Huh?"

He grinned. "I mean, do you need help carrying it."

"Oh, no. It's a puppy."

"A puppy."

"Right, a puppy."

He expelled a stream of air in an exaggerated way, a way that meant he thought a puppy wasn't such a great idea.

I got defensive. "If you can give someone a horse, I can give someone a puppy."

"All right, all right," he said. "Let's bring the puppy in."

"Well, wait," I said. "I want to know about this horse of yours first."

"Why?"

I debated whether I ought to tell him or not. Then I had an idea.

"Wait here," I said. "I want to get something out of the truck."

He looked at me as if I'd gone senile. "Right," he said, "the puppy."

"Not the puppy. Oh, just wait."

I came back with the oil painting, face side away.

"What's that?" he asked.

I turned it toward him as dramatically as I could an object that size.

"Holy shit," he said. "Where'd you get that?"

"From the horse's owner," I said.

"From Dix?"

"Who?"

"Dix. A friend of mine in Oklahoma."

"That's where you got this horse?"

"Robin," he said. "Put that picture down and I'll tell you all about it."

Dix's wife had always wanted a horse. Boots LaRue sold them one. And for what Cody called "a pretty penny," too.

"Then one day Dix called me up," Cody said, "and he was sobbing. The horse had killed his wife, he said. He asked me if I'd take the horse before he ended up putting a bullet in him."

"What did he charge you?"

"Let's not go into that," Cody said. "His wife was dead and he just wanted this horse disappeared."

Wanted this horse *to disappear*, I thought, mentally correcting Cody's grammar. But aloud I said, "And exactly how did this woman die?"

"The horse ran over her. I thought I told you that. The horse is a charger. Runs right for you."

"And what about this video you allegedly have. Did Lola see it?"

He shook his head no about Lola. Then, "It'll make you sick," he said, standing up and walking toward the television.

"You have the actual part where he kills her?"

"No. I have the way he got that way."

"What do you mean?"

"Watch," Cody said, "and see."

What I saw *did* make me sick. It was the know-nothing dead woman actually *training* the horse to charge. And it was unbelievable. I mean, people should have to pass a test before they're allowed to own horses.

Because what this woman had done was go into the pasture with a coffee can filled with some oats. Then she made the horse chase her around for them. And from the way she was laughing, she thought it was really cute.

"You can see," Cody said, "that it wouldn't even take a week before he'd be running right at her."

"Except that she got . . . Well, I hate to say what she deserved, but really—it was what she asked for."

"Yeah."

"So why," I asked, "didn't your friend tell Boots to take the horse back?"

"Oh, well. That's pretty stupid. Apparently, when the horse first started charging, the woman called Boots up as though it was his fault. Threatened to sue him."

Jeez.

And you see stuff like this all the time. Like people who get horses to nip for treats—and the next thing you know, the horse is a savage biter.

But there was no point in telling the grieving husband something like this.

"Why doesn't Dix sue LaRue now? I mean, if they were going to sue him then. . . ?"

"It was the wife who threatened suit. Dix couldn't care less. I don't think he's ever sued anyone in his life." He rewound the tape as he spoke. Then he gestured at the painting. "What about that?"

I told him about Louanne Perry's horse.

"I don't know," he said, looking at the dead Wickingham on canvas. "A lot of horses are marked the same."

"Yeah," I said, "but the hobble thing. The part where they both bend down to drink or graze."

"You don't think two horses could have been hobbled? Or that maybe they're related?"

"No. I think this is the same horse. And admit it—when you saw this painting, that's what you thought, too."

"Oh, sure. But so what? It *couldn't* be the same horse. I mean, if Boots LaRue had been in the picture, that would be one thing, but Boots LaRue—"

"—*is* in the picture," I interrupted. "Because Louanne Perry bought the horse from Boots in the first place."

Cody was shaking his head no, no, no.

"But Boots wasn't anywhere around when the horse *died.* Don't you get it?"

"I get it," I said. "But I believe what I believe all the same."

I'm stubborn that way, I guess. But I was mad about Ornell Standish saying whatever he'd said. And if the horse was alive, I was off the hook.

"Fortunately," Cody said, "you can't prove it."

"What do you mean, 'Fortunately'?" I asked.

"Because if you're right," Cody said, "Lola will lose the horse to Louanne Perry."

"But if I'm right, Boots LaRue and Ornell Standish will go to jail."

Cody started laughing. It was a rollicking kind of laugh, a laugh that kept getting bigger as it went along. It finally ended with Cody gasping for breath.

"What's so funny?" I asked him.

"Who the hell is this Ornett character?" he said. "Talking to you is like being led blindfolded through a maze."

"Ornell," I said. "Not Ornett."

And for some reason, that got him going again. He was *still* laughing when I came back in with the puppy. "His nickname is Rooney," I said. "His full name is The Macaroon." I put the puppy down on the floor.

The puppy sniffed around as if he wanted to pee.

Cody and I collided as we bent to pick him up. While we apologized to each other, the puppy squatted.

"I'll get the paper towel," Cody said. "You take that fellow outside for a spell."

I drove back to our farm thinking not about the horse situation, but about that kitchen of ours. How on earth would I ever get it clean? And what about the puppy? Would I be able to housebreak him? Would he chew the slippers I was going to buy for Jeet? How about the purple socks? Why had I complicated my life this way? And what was I going to do about Lola's horse? Let it drop? Or keep on checking until—who knew?

When I came up the lane, I saw a strange car in the spot where Jeet's was ordinarily parked.

In my present frame of mind, I assumed this couldn't auger well.

Could Boots LaRue, or Standish, or someone have gotten wind about the questions I'd been asking about the horse? And could they have come to silence me? I mean, in one of those noir detective novels, that's what it would mean.

In my case, however, it probably meant that the Mormons were canvassing the neighborhood and wanted to talk to me about salvation.

Well, I could use a little salvation, I thought, gunning the truck and then sliding to a stop.

A woman I had never seen before was standing at the front door. She didn't look like she was out proselytizing because she wasn't dressed up at all. She was wearing an outfit that looked familiar. A sort of ninja-like pants and tunic thing.

I racked my brain even as I smiled at her.

She scowled back.

Great. Just what the doctor ordered. Probably an angry Avon lady or something.

CHAPTER 8

After the way I'd driven in, you'd think she'd have bolted. Or that I would have leaped from the truck and run full tilt toward her, but I didn't.

No.

Instead, I steeled myself for whatever it was. She evidently did the same.

I continued looking at her outfit, wondering why I felt I had seen it before.

Meanwhile, the woman frowned more deeply than before and said, "Merry Christmas."

"Merry Christmas," I said warily.

"I am Teresa," the woman told me. "I have this." She handed me an envelope with my mother's handwriting on it; it was addressed to "Dearest Robin and Jeet."

I opened it.

"I hope you won't miss the annual fruitcake," my mom had written, "but I wanted to give you something a little different this year. Something you might really need. So—and I hope you won't be offended, Robin, dear—here is Teresa. She's a wonderful housekeeper, and she's yours for a day or even a few, however long you need her."

Then there was a P.S., which said, underlined, *"Within reason!"*

The outfit. Of course. It was one of my mother's castoffs. In fact, the last time I'd seen my mother, she'd been wearing it.

I looked at Teresa. "Well, what . . . ?" I began, not knowing what I ought to ask her.

Teresa solved the problem nicely. "I clean," she said. She gestured at her feet, where for the first time I noticed a bucket with a pile of rags inside.

Boy, had she come to the right place.

I unlocked the door and let the kitchen speak for itself. I swear, she took a step backward and gulped before managing a weak smile and a nod and rolling up her sleeves. She was muttering something.

"What?" I asked her.

"Your mother," Teresa said. "She told me be prepared for hay, for horse manure, stuff like that. She didn't say nothing about this." She indicated the kitchen with a sweeping gesture.

"I have never had horse manure in the kitchen," I countered. "I always take my boots off outside if they're dirty. And I shake the hay off out there, too."

Teresa glared at me all the same.

I debated about what I ought to do. Before I'd even decided, my fingers had dialed Houston information and I was writing down the number of Boots LaRue.

Except that, when I called there, I was told by someone—his Teresa, probably—that the LaRues were unable to come to the phone because they were busy getting ready to spend the holidays visiting relatives.

"Where?" I asked.

There was a loud *tsk*. "In California."

"Hollywood? Los Angeles?" I asked.

"Burbank."

Burbank. Wasn't that close to L.A.? I mean, hadn't Johnny Carson made all those Burbank jokes, and hadn't all his guests talked about being in L.A., which would mean that it was pretty close? Close enough to be practically the same thing?

Except that Johnny Carson hadn't been on the tube in years. Maybe I remembered it wrong. And anyway, that was hardly the way one's geographical knowledge ought to be gleaned.

I called the L.A. area code and asked for Ornell Standish, but found out that there wasn't any such person there. In the Burbank area code, however, they had him listed. I not only got the phone number, but the address.

Ha! What could this mean?

I sat slumped at the desk and drummed my fingers against the stack of magazines thereon.

That's when Teresa saved the day.

"I hear you on the phone," she said.

"Yeah," I answered disconsolately.

She walked past me and picked up the paper on which I'd written Ornell Standish's address.

She was from the L.A. area, she said. It was a hop, skip, and a jump from the Burbank airport to just about anywhere in Burbank. "Here, especially," she said, pointing to where I'd written "Hollywood Way."

"Five, ten minutes," she said.

"Yeah? Well, I don't see how I could go," I told her. "My husband is out of town, and there are the horses . . . "

"Is good that your husband is gone. And the horses," she said, "I take care of them for you gladly."

I looked up at her. She was right. With Jeet out of the way, I was in the clear for a couple of days at least. And I had Teresa available to feed Plum and Spier. What was more, I had a present for Jeet, in the form of a Jack Russell Terrier puppy. And I even had a present for Lola and Cody, in the form of that painting.

There was still my mom, but she was used to me being late. And anyway, I could charge some flowers or something and take care of that. So I had. . . ?

I fished into my pocket and extracted the wad of bills I'd saved for Christmas presents. I had $182.50.

Fare to L.A.

Where I could seek out Ornell Standish and maybe even Boots LaRue—and, at the very least, I could tell Ornell Standish that I didn't appreciate him going around telling people that Louanne Perry's horse had died while I was taking care of him . . . and whatever else the man was out there saying. And I could also confirm—or else get rid of—this nagging feeling that I had about Lola's horse.

Like did Noel have a full brother? Or had some hanky-panky gone on? If it had, my presence alone ought to spark some kind of reaction, right? Even if I didn't act on anything I learned, it would comfort me one heck of a lot to know, once and for all, what had happened.

So I took Teresa outside and told her the ins and outs of horse feeding, including the caveats about how they can't vomit, so feeding properly is very, very, *very* important.

And the image of Wickie flashed through my mind. Not that I'd fed him incorrectly, but that he'd died of a colic, and a colic is often directly related to . . .

Except, wait a minute. Wickie was alive. At least I thought that he was alive, and by some slippery and highly illegal shenanigans, he was now in the stable of my best friend.

Of course, baldly stated that way, it sounded pretty unlikely.

Less unlikely, I reminded myself, is that *two* horses who looked *exactly* alike should turn out to have been hobbled.

He's alive, I decided. I liked that scenario a whole lot better.

And Cody's point—that Lola could end up losing the horse—didn't really hold any water, because Louanne wouldn't *want* the horse back—because she was into dogs now. If, however, she ended up wanting him, everybody involved, even Cody's chum in Oklahoma, would have to pay everybody else, kind of like a chain letter, and it would all even out in the end.

And for that matter, ha! I wouldn't put it past Ornell Standish to have even charged Louanne for playing knacker and hauling off the "corpse"—so she could just sue him and probably end up better off.

But she wouldn't want money because she'd been paid by the insurance company, and she probably wouldn't want to open that particular can of worms, so that was another point in Lola's favor.

So I would be doing this . . . why?

To restore my good name, even if it had been besmirched in the eyes of only one or two people. To bring about justice.

* * *

Except there was no justice; I already knew that. I mean, if there were justice, I'd be taller, thinner, and a better rider. I mean, I deserve that.

So scratch justice.

The truth was, I'd be doing this to get Wickie's death off my conscience. It didn't bother me all the time, but I did think about it off and on. I did wonder if there had been anything at all I might have done to keep him from dying. And I did refuse, and intended to keep on refusing, to ever feed in someone's—except for Lola's—absence as a result.

Plus I would like to see Ornell Standish's face when I turned up.

And I don't even know why that was. It could be because I felt he'd done poor Louanne Perry, who knew next to nothing about horses, a terrible injustice getting her to buy all those high-powered horses, and there I'd be, like a conscience. I mean, Louanne—just like the poor woman in Oklahoma who was now dead—should have started out with lesser horses, horses who were broken to death, horses to learn from.

Okay, I'm preaching and ranting again, and I'll stop.

I'll stop especially because Teresa was proffering the newspaper classifieds and tugging on my sleeve. And saying, here, in the transportation column of the *Austin Daily Progress* itself, was someone selling a ticket to and from Burbank dated tomorrow.

Tomorrow. Sunday. Four days before Christmas.

I didn't see any reason why I couldn't do that, so I called the person and negotiated a $120 price.

That would leave me $62.50 to cab around and maybe eat.

I hollered into the kitchen, asking Teresa if she thought $62.50 would be enough, and got a wavy kind of yes. But she made me promise to put $20 extra in my jeans pocket just to be on the safe side.

This she lent me.

I called Cody and tried my plan out on him. He, of course, thought it was dopey all around. And not only dopey but pointless.

I laid it on thick about how vindicating myself vis-à-vis Wickingham's death would help my faltering self-esteem.

"The day your self-esteem falters," he answered, "is the day I'll end up"—he paused, trying to think of something really far-fetched—"falling in love with you," he said.

Well.

Jeet fell in love with me.

And there were several—well, maybe a couple of—fellows before Jeet who had done the same.

But there wasn't any time to tell him all of this. Because all I wanted from him was a pledge that he'd drive me to the airport.

I know, you're wondering why I didn't drive myself, but believe me, the airport parking spots are designed for teeny little cars. I would need six parking spaces side by side to get my truck in there. Well, okay. That's an exaggeration. I'd need two. But you could never find two together, take my word for it. Sometimes you could drive around for half an hour hoping to find one.

Plus, with Cody driving me, I wouldn't have to be sidetracked worrying about whether or not a one-day trip would mean the short-term or long-term parking lot.

"What am I supposed to tell Lola?" Cody asked.

"About what?"

"About taking you someplace at the crack of dawn."

Well, actually, my flight left a little later than that.

"I don't know. You can think of something. I mean, you could tell her the truth—that you're taking me to the airport. And that will mean that you can tell her the truth about picking me up, too." And I gave him the time I'd be getting in.

"But what do I tell her about why you're going?" he asked.

I thought for a long while. "Well, don't tell her I'm going to L.A. then. Tell her I'm going to El Paso. For—I don't know—a conjugal visit with Jeet."

Cody laughed.

I fumed. Did he find the idea of having a conjugal visit with me funny? And far-fetched? "What are you laughing about?" I demanded.

He ignored my question. "I'll tell her you're spending the day with Jeet," he said. "Or I won't say it's you I'm taking. I'll just say a friend."

"How's my puppy? The Macaroon?" I changed the subject.

"Obsessed with his ball," Cody said. "You'll have to buy one of those pitching machines."

"Has he peed in the house anymore? Or chewed anything?"

"He has peed out of doors twice. And, like I said, the only thing he's interested in chewing is that ball of his."

I smiled, picturing his alert little brown-and-white presence.

"Do you think Jeet will like him?" I asked, and got a yes. But then Cody returned to the present problem.

"So do you have your ticket or what?" he asked.

"I found a used one in the transportation column." Actually Teresa had, but I didn't want to have to explain who she was, et cetera, so it didn't seem unethical to take the credit myself. "I have to go to the Rio Central Apartments in Austin and pick it up."

"The Rio Central Apartments?" Cody screamed. "Don't you ever watch the news?" he asked me. "That's a terrible place." He proceeded to tell me about drive-by shootings and various other activities he'd known to have happened there. "In fact, that ticket—if there is a ticket—was probably purchased to consummate some drug deal."

Can you believe how many alarmists there are in the world?

But in this case, Cody was truly concerned. I ended up agreeing to let *him* drive to wherever it was and buy the ticket for me.

"But listen," I said. "Since Jeet isn't here, could the puppy maybe come over for a little while?"

So there I am, on the bedroom floor, tugging the end of one of Jeet's old socks while Rooney growls and shakes his head, tugging on the other.

This is when Teresa chooses to accost me.

"No dogs," she said, prying Rooney's teeth from the sock and lifting him expertly. "I clean up after people. I do not clean after dogs."

"It's just for a couple of hours," I say. "Until Cody gets back."

She is not appeased. She is, in fact, still holding a

grudge about the tortilla debacle. "I have never in my lifetime seen a kitchen like yours," she says.

I smile wryly, apologetically, wondering what Jeet, had he seen the room, would have thought. I mean, he knows I'm not much of a housekeeper, but still, this kitchen was on a level with—I don't know—taking a hunk of cheese out of the fridge and finding teeth marks on it or something.

"Your mother," Teresa went on, "she tell me not to expect to find spic and span. But hey, *caramba*!" She shook her head fiercely. Rooney watched her, then boosted himself high enough to lick her cheek.

Teresa giggled.

"He likes you," I pointed out.

Teresa giggled again. The dog had won her over. "A couple of hours." She put the pup down on the floor again. He eyed her ankle. She was wearing nylons, I noted. I hoped he wouldn't go for them. "Okay," she said.

I called Jeet's hotel in El Paso. He was actually there. "I got your message," I said. "About doing a tamale thing, too."

"Are you feeling okay?" he asked, which was not quite a good response to my tamale remark, but that's the way marriage goes.

"Why wouldn't I?"

"Because there was an allergist sitting next to me on the plane," he said. "You ought to have Cedar Fever big time."

"Cody gave me something. Headache powder. It worked."

Usually I took a bunch of antihistamine slash cold medicine stuff. You know what I mean, the old "*plop, plop, fizz, fizz*" thing.

Rooney came clicking down the hall, looking for me. "You're going to love your Christmas present," I said, thinking maybe I should buy one of those nail trimmers and cut the little booger's nails a bit. At this rate, Jeet would hear him, and that would spoil the surprise.

I held the phone squished against my shoulder with my chin and picked the puppy up.

"So what are you going to do while I'm gone?" Jeet asked.

"Miss you," I said, thinking it was just as well not to mention my California jaunt. "Just sit around the house and mope because I'm missing you."

"That'll be the day," Jeet said, but the little laugh he gave as much as said, *Good answer*.

So now all I had left to do was cancel the riding lesson I had with Wanda, who you maybe already know is my psychic riding instructor.

Of course, you may wonder why I had to cancel it, since, being psychic, she ought to have known—but still . . .

And anyway, I have learned not to ask questions like these.

I have also learned to trust her cryptic—nay—inexplicable messages. They all seem to sort of make sense after the fact, like horoscopes.

I called to find that, though it was only midday, Wanda had eggnogged herself beyond cryptic, beyond even inexplicable. Wanda had eggnogged herself into *The Twilight Zone*.

"Oooh," she said coyly. "Bubbelah, you won't believe what Santa is going to do for you."

"Do?" I said. "You mean bring, don't you? What Santa is going to bring for me?"

A long pause. Then a relatively sober, "No, *do*. Do." Then, "This is Robern Varn, isn't it?"

"Right. Robin Vaughan."

"Then"—she was emphatic—"it's *do*."

"I have to cancel my lesson," I said, wondering what said lesson, given her current state, might have entailed.

"No problem," she said. "Merry . . . uh . . . " She was trying to think of the holiday, I could tell. She was saved by hiccuping.

"Listen," I said, "same to you."

I'd just hung up when the phone rang again. It was Lola.

"Have you seen Cody?" she asked.

"I, uh . . . " I said.

"Well, have you or haven't you?" she demanded.

"Well, uh . . . yes. He, uh . . . went someplace." Then the puppy licked me and I sort of giggled.

"Like where?"

"I, uh . . . " God, it's a good thing I don't work for the CIA.

"Robin," she said, "do you know where Cody is or not?"

"Not."

"Have you been drinking wine or something? Or taking those antihistamines?"

She usually asked if I'd been out in the sun, but since it was December . . . I tried to change the subject. "Listen," I asked her, "did you watch the video Cody wanted you to watch? The one where the woman all but teaches that horse to charge?"

"No," Lola said. "It's practically Christmas. Some of us don't have a lot of free time."

Oh, right. I put the puppy down, mostly so I could

sound as stern as I felt I needed to. "Well, some of us," I said pointedly, "are a lot less crabby than others."

There was a long silence. Then Lola said, "I'm sorry."

"Okay," I told her. But I couldn't resist making her feel a trifle more guilty. "And maybe Cody's off doing something Christmas-y," I said.

"Aah," Lo said. "I see."

The puppy picked up his little ball and tossed it—and I think I squealed a little.

"What was that?" Lo asked.

"You'll see."

"My present, you mean?"

"No, Jeet's present. I got him a puppy."

"Oh, Lord," she said.

"Well you got a horse," I said defensively.

"I know. But Jeet doesn't seem the puppy type."

"What is that supposed to mean?"

"Let me get this straight," Lola said. "You're the uncrabby one, is that right?"

We both laughed and said good-bye.

CHAPTER 9

Do I look like an Orlando Washington to you? Because that was the name on my ticket—and no one at the counter in Austin when I checked in, or, indeed, anywhere, so much as batted an eye. In fact, the woman there didn't seem to want to hear the story I'd concocted about how my mother was an unstoppable Virginia Woolf fan.

Maybe the airlines are used to people traveling under assumed names. Maybe, in fact, the way they issue nonrefundable tickets has even prompted same.

Orlando Washington.

If the plane had crashed, that's how I'd have gone down in the roll books. Except that Cody, postmortem, would have set the record straight.

But, of course, the plane didn't crash, even though it had to land in Phoenix and take off again. On purpose, I mean. And you know how that's the most dangerous time. I stared out the window at the mountains and they looked like papier-mâché. If we had to make an emergency landing, I told myself, it would be soft.

The minute we were on the ground I wanted out of that capsule and into what I think of as pure air.

Airport air.

I pulled out one of the little paper packages of those headache powders—I'd managed to score two, you'll recall, from Cody—and wondered where I could get a cup.

A concessionaire was glad to sell me one—he charged me a quarter for it. I stood at a water fountain, pouring the powder into the liquid, then stirring with my finger.

I saw someone I remembered from the plane watching me.

Not a sinister someone. A jolly-faced, gray-haired guy.

I smiled.

He smiled back. Then he went off to a bank of pay phones.

I went outside and contemplated the huge saguaro cacti the airport had used in its landscaping scheme.

They don't grow near where I live or anywhere in Texas, although I've seen them on dust jackets of books that are supposed to be set here. They looked massive, ancient, protective.

I got back on the plane—a different one, because my original flight was going on to San Jose—and went immediately to the emergency exit.

This is where I always elect to huddle, engulfed in terror as I envision horrible, flaming eventualities.

This time, however, I didn't have a chance to do that, being chatted up instead by the very same jolly-looking man I'd seen before.

He arrived dramatically, too, since originally I—or should I say Orlando—was slated to sit next to a woman who was so huge that she'd reserved both of the seats beside me.

I know, I'm not supposed to feel this way about someone handicapped by blubber, but she was so enormously fat, she'd been boarded first.

I mean, it must have been quite something, too, shoehorning her up the narrow little passageway.

Anyway, when I came up the aisle, there she was. Except at the very last minute, and over protests that seemed to exhaust the poor woman, it turned out she was in one of the seats that the old guy had reserved. "I paid for these seats," she said, crossing her arms and looking as though she was going to make the stewardess, who had informed her of the mix-up, move her, which probably would have been impossible.

But then the man spoke to her himself, sotto voce, and the fat woman looked a tad flustered and said okay.

Still, it delayed the flight about twenty minutes because, as I said, they didn't need one seat for her but two, and in order to find two together, a lot of seat switching had to transpire.

They ended up moving the fat woman up to first class.

Everyone on the plane was amused, but we all knew that we had to keep from laughing.

Jolly sat down beside me, tittered, and rolled his eyes conspiratorially.

I allowed myself a little grin. "So what did you say to her?" I asked.

"I told her I'd see that she got something nice in her stocking," he answered, winking.

And that's when I realized how much he looked like Santa Claus. Without the beard, of course.

I guess I said so.

I know, if I were a politically correct individual, I

would have been offended by the wink instead, but you know from the fat lady episode that I'm not. In fact, if you really want to know, I actually watch *Married with Children* reruns. And you guessed it, every single time Al Bundy makes a fat woman joke, I crack up.

Except that, in addition, Jolly, whose name is Nicholas, by the way, is so harmless looking. He has a twin brother who's an actor and a model.

"My brother's playing Santa on Merry Christmas billboards all over California," he tells me. The brother's a character actor, Nicholas elaborates, explaining the difference between this and leading man roles.

"And what about you?" I asked him. "What kind of job do you have?"

"Oh," he said, "let's not talk about me. Let's find out about you."

So now that it was my turn, I told him I was going out to see a man about a horse.

"Indeed," Nicholas said, looking enormously interested. "Horse."

"Right," I said. "Horse."

"And what sort of man?" Nicholas asked.

"A vet," I said.

"A veteran." His eyes were twinkling merrily. "Vietnam?"

"Oh, no." I laughed. "A vet to me is a veterinarian. It's this guy, Ornell Standish. He—"

Then Nicholas asked, interrupting, "Why would a veterinarian be open this close to Christmas?"

Which, naturally, I hadn't thought of. It was Sunday. So what was I going to do if his office was closed? "He's Jewish?" I tried.

"Someone named Standish is Jewish?" Nicholas ventured.

"Okay, how about he's dedicated." I tried again, though I knew that, if what I suspected about Standish was even remotely true, he wasn't at all. So I guessed again. "Ha!" I said. "I know. He's married to a shrew and the office is the only place where he can get away from her."

"Could be," Nicholas said. He whipped out a tiny notebook and said he'd look Standish's address up while I did whatever I had to do in the ladies' room at the airport when we landed. Maybe he could drop me off there.

"I already know the address," I said. "It's on Hollywood Way."

Nicholas returned to talking about his brother. His brother, he told me, knew how to ride. He took lessons at the Los Angeles Equestrian Center for a role he once had in a Western. Nicholas didn't even notice how I cringed when he said that, because if there's anything I hate, it's those Westerns, where everybody practically yanks his horse over backward in order to stop.

Anyway, we chatted amiably until we got to Nicholas's car, a no-frills gray sedan. I guess I was disappointed, because I'd heard that in California, the car is king. I got over it, though. I mean, a ride is a ride.

All the way out to Hollywood Way, my mouth was watering. Because after we'd passed the clutter of tiny houses, we got into one of tiny businesses. Restaurants, a lot of them. Ethnic, too. Mexican, Japanese, even Hungarian. On the plane, we had only been offered nuts.

But Nicholas never indicated that he was hungry,

and me, I was so glad to be saving money by not having to take a taxi that I didn't dare.

"Do you want me to wait for you?" Nicholas asked as we pulled up in front of the palm-ringed stucco clinic that had Standish's name in front of it.

There were cars there, so obviously it was open, too.

"I don't know," I said. "That might look suspicious."

Nick stared at me, wide-eyed. "Isn't going in there without an animal suspicious?" he asked. He'd have made a great detective.

I frowned. "Well, I don't know." I was sort of squirming by this time. I mean, I had this feeling that Nicholas was, I don't know, sort of toying with me. But I told myself that all I had to do was level with him. Tell him the entire story—beginning with Louanne and her crazy notions—and then bring him up to the present.

So I said, "Okay. Since we're sort of partners in crime right now, I'd better tell you everything."

And Nicholas leaned back in his seat, smiled smugly, and shut the engine off. "Good idea," he said.

"Here's what's going on," I said, launching into the story.

Midway through, he had a glazed look, a look that seemed worse than the one Jeet always got when a long story with a lot of horse stuff in it began to unspool.

"Are you all right?" I asked him. "Because if you're not, I have this headache powder that will fix you right up." I reached into the back pocket of my jeans and pulled it out.

"Headache powder?" he asked.

I laughed. "They're pretty old-fashioned," I said, as if I were an expert instead of a new convert to the medication. "Sort of like powdered aspirin. My theory is that they work faster because they're already dissolved. You know. They don't have to melt."

He took the powder packet and tucked it in his own pocket. "As a matter of fact," he said, "I just remembered an appointment downtown."

"Wait," I told him, wanting to finish my story. "This really gets good. Because, see, I'm not really Orlando Washington," which is what I'd told him initially. "I just saw this ticket advertised in the transportation section of the newspaper. I'm really Robin Vaughan and—"

"You bought a ticket out of the newspaper?" he asked. "The transportation column? You mean in the classifieds?"

"Uh-huh," I said proudly.

"It's been nice to meet you, Robin," he said wearily. "Really. It's been lovely. And I'm glad I was able to help you come this far, but I've got to run. Really. I've . . . " He started the engine and looked as though he was about to reach across me to fling the door on my side open so that he could push me out.

Well.

I can take a hint.

I drew myself up and thanked him—and even would have shaken his hand if it had been offered. "I was going to take a cab anyway," I said. "So it's no big deal." Still, though, I felt sort of stung. But after all, he was just some stranger, really. But even so, as he drove away I felt like yelling that he ought to invest in an ejector passenger seat.

I honestly don't know why I was taking it so hard,

except that it was rejection, after all. Sudden and cruel and unwarranted rejection.

I stood there as he drove off into—well, not the sunset. It was early. And I couldn't actually see the sun through the legendary smog.

I walked up to the clinic. There was a choice to be made. The cat entrance was to the left and the dog entrance to the right.

There were imitation holly wreaths on both of the doors.

I tried to work myself into a Christmas-y frame of mind, but I was still smarting from having bored Nicholas into abandoning me, and, at this point, my entire mission seemed pretty dumb.

I considered going through neither door. What I really considered was walking until I could find a taxi to take me back to the airport—to wait for Orlando's flight home.

Boy. I almost wish I had.

CHAPTER 10

Why *am* I doing this? I asked myself, as I pushed in through CATS. And I don't really have an answer, except that I was already there, so I figured I might as well let Dr. Ornell Standish know it. In fact, his reaction to my name ought to tell me something.

But what?

And what if I did look into the man's rheumy red eyes and see guilt? What would I say? Would I say, I know that Wickie really didn't die?

And he'd say, Listen, you fool. Wickie had a brother.

I mean, Nicholas had a brother. Brothers are not uncommon, either in the human or the equine world.

But still, I *was* there, and I felt like crap—because I blamed myself even if no one else did. I mean, Wickie died, I thought, on my watch.

And Standish did tell Len Reasoner . . . and God only knows who else. And if I was reading what Louanne had said correctly, he had practically implied that Wickie's death was my fault.

Unless I was being paranoid. I mean, I tried to recall exactly what Standish was alleged to have said but couldn't at the moment.

But even worse, I was thinking: Horses *do* look

alike, a lot of them, and brown isn't really an unusual color—and hell, for all I know, horses that come from Mexico and below have all been hobbled and fold up like that to graze and drink.

Except I'd seen dozens of horses from Mexico, and not a-one of them ever did that. Plus I'd seen horses *in* Mexico and they didn't. Even the poorest horse owners had erected fences of some sort. Or else they tethered them.

Then a white-coated person—a woman—stood up and asked if she could help me.

"I'd like to see Dr. Standish," I said.

"In reference to. . . ?" She waited.

I was about to say that I was an old acquaintance of his from Texas, but I realized in the nick of time that that would be tipping my hand too quickly. Then a Len Reasoner–inspired idea flashed at me. "I understand he sees a lot of movie stars' horses and I want to write about it. In a magazine."

"Do you have an assignment?" she asked, looking very superior all of a sudden.

"Yes," I said.

"And from whom?" she asked.

"From *Horse Chat*," I said, naming a magazine I'd just made up.

Her brow furrowed.

So I said, "I also have an in with the *Austin Daily Progress*." Well, I did—if you want to count Jeet's job.

"May I have your name?"

I almost said Orlando Washington, because I'd been hammering at myself to remember to use that name during my whole trip. But at the last minute, I told her it was Robin Vaughan.

"Oh." She brightened. "That sounds familiar."

"Thanks."

She picked up the phone and dialed a couple of numbers, then turned away from me.

She had one of those voices. You know what I mean. She could carry on a whole conversation on the phone and I couldn't hear a word she was saying—even though I was standing right there.

I, personally, do not have one of those voices. If I try to adopt one, the other person can't hear me and keeps asking me to repeat. So I boom right off the bat.

Anyway, before she hung up, a door in the rear creaked open and I saw, I swear, the eye of Ornell Standish himself looking me over.

And sure enough, seconds after it creaked shut, the receptionist told me it would be quite some time before Dr. Standish was free.

"How long, about?" I asked.

She dithered around on that one, not expecting me, I guess, to ask. "Half an hour or so," she said.

"I'll wait," I said. Then, in a burst of inspiration, I asked, "How about Boots LaRue? Is he here?"

She looked thoughtful. She turned to her computer and pushed a few buttons. "No," she said. "No patient by that name."

I laughed, but I thought she had given me the answer anyway. It was no, right? "No," I said. "Boots LaRue is a person. A relative of Dr. Standish's, I think."

Although even that was sounding like a mighty big assumption right now. God. I had spent all this money—and traipsed to Los Angeles or Burbank or who knows where I was—in vain.

No wonder I was practically always ending up in trouble.

"I really need to use your bathroom," I said, which, all of a sudden, I did.

"We don't have a public bathroom," she said.

"A private one is fine," I told her.

She looked at me suspiciously. As though she thought that, once behind the creaky door, I was going to storm Ornell Standish's office or something.

So I looked the way that little Jack Russell Terrier had, kind of doe-eyed, head cocked to one side. "Please?" I begged.

"Oh, okay," she said, leading me to the creaky door and opening it.

A thickly medicinal smell washed over me.

"Third door on the left," she said.

It really wasn't a public bathroom. In fact, judging from the stacks of cardboard boxes that were in there with me, it was half their bathroom and half their storeroom.

And it was their locker room, too. I mean, clothes were hanging off hooks as if this was the place where people changed. Even Ornell Standish himself appeared to change here, and he hadn't altered his fashion sense, either—because it was that very same white suit I'd first seen him in at Louanne's.

He was wearing scrubs now, so maybe he really was busy, spaying bitches or something. I'd seen that flash of scrub green when he peered in at me through the creaking door.

I reached for my fanny pack in order to hang it up and—Oh, my God. It wasn't there! I took my jeans down and sank onto the toilet bowl, ransacking my memory.

Was it in Nicholas's car?

But it couldn't be, not unless it had fallen off.

Was Nicholas a thief who had surreptitiously cut the strap that held it to my body? I'd heard of thieves doing that.

Naw.

The last time I clearly remembered having it was in the Burbank airport. In the bathroom. Just like now.

I'd taken the fanny pack off and I'd hung it on the hook on the toilet stall door. But surely I wouldn't have left it there!

Except that I was always leaving things places, and I probably had done just that.

Along with my return plane ticket and all but twenty dollars of my cash. Teresa's twenty dollars.

I had yet another internal debate, this time over whether or not I'd ever get the fanny pack back. It was the Christmas season, and that would make whoever found it predisposed to be extra nice. Plus, if I'd found it, I'd have turned it in.

Unless whoever found it figured I'd be coming right back and left it there. What were the chances of two honest people in a row turning up?

One time at our local dressage club meeting, a new woman sitting next to me left her purse. I was going to take it back up to the counter, but then I remembered that she'd said she lived out toward us and so I took it home, thinking it would be easier for her to get it from me than have to drive all the way into Austin for it.

When I got home, I tried to call her, but something was wrong with our phone—and in the morning, it was still out of order. I drove over to

Lola's and called—and the woman's husband answered and was *furious*!

It turned out, the woman had just gone to the bathroom, and when she'd come out, both her purse and I had disappeared.

She'd had to spend the night in Austin because her car keys were in the purse. And when she'd tried to call me, a recording said the phone was temporarily out of service.

The only good news is that I mentioned to a couple of people that I was taking the purse home with me. Otherwise, she'd have thought I'd stolen it, I guess.

And the whole thing was made even worse by the fact that she was a dressage judge—an "r"—and I had to ride in front of her at a lot of schooling shows. Not that she took it out on me. It's just that I would see her and get very nervous remembering how mad her husband had been, and I'd blow things I ordinarily would have aced.

Oh, well.

One other time, I was at the gym with Lola and she'd gotten dressed before I did and gone out on the floor, and—well, you guessed it—there on the bench was her purse.

I graciously put it into my locker so that it wouldn't get stolen, and when I went back into the locker room for something I'd forgotten, all hell had broken loose because it hadn't been Lola's purse at all. It had been someone else's, and, of course, the someone else thought it had been stolen.

"Oh, God" I'd said, laughing and unlocking my locker and handing it back to her. She'd snatched it away without even cracking a smile. As though I'd really meant to steal it or something.

So anyway, I'd probably get my fanny pack back, I decided. I had only to call the airport. Someone who was very much like me had no doubt turned it in.

I ignored the little argumentative voice that was saying, *Fat chance.*

Except that, meanwhile, what was I going to do for money and a plane ride back to Texas? Because if I didn't get it back, whoever had that plane ticket would be practicing being Orlando Washington by now.

I went through all I could remember again, and yes, I had a very definite memory of taking it off and hanging it on the hook—and absolutely no memory of having buckled it back on.

Just then the speaker system at Standish's office, which had been piping violin-laden versions of what ought to be jingly, peppy carols into the room, shifted to the spoken word. "In this season of giving, let us know what we can do for you . . . " said an oily voice of indeterminate gender.

That's the spirit. That's what everyone would be thinking. So of course my fanny pack would be returned to me. But just in case . . .

I pulled up my jeans, eyeing that white suit of Standish's. Yeah, there was something he could do for me. I reached into the trousers' pocket. Voilà! A wallet.

I flipped through it. Zippo in the money department. But there was a stash of credit cards, too: Visa, MasterCard, American Express, National Tire Wholesalers. My fingers trembled. It would be so easy! Except that it would make me a common thief.

No. I could take only one.

Then I'd be borrowing, not stealing.

In fact, I could legitimately take *all* of the cards. Because the credit cards could serve as part of my investigation. I mean, most people don't pay cash for things, and maybe finding out what Standish had purchased could tell me something, right? Like maybe Ornell Standish had treated Boots LaRue to a Houston-Burbank flight. Then I'd have more proof they were in cahoots.

Also, what if the cards could prove that Ornell Standish and Boots LaRue got together regularly? I mean, what if Standish traveled to Houston? Wouldn't that cinch—well, maybe not everything—but something?

And how would I find that out? By calling MasterCard, Visa, and American Express to see if there had been any airline tickets charged. Which I'd need the cards to do.

And while I was at it, I could also use the cards to eat . . . and maybe even fly back home.

I'd reimburse Standish, of course.

But meanwhile, my problem, if I had one, was solved.

But wait a minute. What do they ask you when you call those credit card places? I mean, if I were legitimately going to track down stuff about Standish's credit history, what would I need? The expiration date, which is on the card, but also his zip code.

I pulled the wallet back out and fished around for one of the business cards I'd seen.

It was his, all right, but it didn't have an address. Only various phone numbers. Office.

Beeper. Emergency. I pocketed it anyway, but I still needed the zip.

Aha! A label off one of the boxes in the storeroom would do. And if that was wrong, I'd try adjoining zip numbers. Surely he lived near here somewhere. And as for blundering around, not really knowing the zip and all, it wasn't as though some live person was going to hear me trying this and that and assume I was a great master criminal. It's machines you deal with when you call the credit card companies. You just punch in numbers.

So I pocketed the cards, congratulating myself for exhibiting, I thought, a certain genius for self-justification.

I only hoped the mood would last. Because in some people's book, I might just *be* a common thief.

So okay, as I left the little room there was another debate raging inside my skull. Would the receptionist take one look at me and know what I had done?

Oh, God. What if they had cameras in there, the way they do at banks and 7-Elevens! I decided, however, to brazen it through.

"So," I said upon emerging, "is Dr. Standish ready yet?"

"I told you it would be at least half an hour," she said.

"Oh." I looked at my watch. "Hasn't it been?" Then I played on her sympathy. "Listen," I told her, "I've got to make a call. I've just discovered something awful."

"Local?"

"I don't know," I admitted. "I've got to call the airport. I left my fanny pack there."

"At LAX?" she asked.

I shook my head no. "Burbank," I told her.

She rolled her eyes. "Well, either way, good luck," she said, pointedly indicating that she didn't think there was a chance in hell that I'd retrieve it.

But she listened intently to my end of the phone call as I got switched around. I even saw some concern written on her face.

Finally a very wonderful someone at the airport said yes, indeed, my fanny pack was there all right.

I gave Standish's receptionist a thumbs-up sign as she handed me a pencil so that I could write down the room I had to go to in order to reclaim it.

"God," she said, impressed. "And here comes Dr. Standish. This must be your lucky day."

He was in his suit now—the suit from which I'd stolen his credit cards—and he was beaming at me, which probably meant he didn't know me from Adam.

And that was good, for now.

But the effort of greeting me made him redden and perspire. Because, if anything, he was more porcine than ever.

Oh, he may have purchased larger clothes, though in the very same color and style. It's just that he had, once again, grown beyond their capacity. And, once again, he was in denial about acknowledging it.

But hey. Who was I to talk? Hadn't I, just about a month ago, had to zip my jeans up by flattening myself on the mattress and using pliers to tug the zipper up? And hadn't I stood ever so carefully, hoping that said zipper would hold? And hadn't I walked with itty-bitty steps to the full-length mirror—only to discover that I was mushroomed out over said jeans at the waist in a way that was, well, hideous?

Except that I'd gone to the Wal-Mart that very day and purchased a larger pair. *His* clothes—Standish's—were still too small for him. I guess that made him an optimist, but in terms of looking halfway decent as you wend your way through life, being a realist would have been a lot better.

"Miss Clemson here"—he waved in the direction of the reception desk—"says you're a writer. She says you're doing an article for *Horse Chat.*"

Everybody wants publicity, I thought. Everybody. "About the movie stars you deal with," I said easily. I guess after pocketing someone's credit cards, a little thing like a lie amounts to zip. "And, of course, their horses."

Your motives are excellent, the good angel on my shoulder all but shouted in my ear. *Plus you'll repay him.* And who knows, maybe I'd actually write an article and sell it for exactly enough to pay him back.

"I'm on my way to the Los Angeles Equestrian Center now," he said. "Would you like to go along?"

"If you're driving," I said, figuring this was turning out far better than I'd expected.

He led me to one of those zippy BMW two-seaters. The kind that cost more than our whole Primrose Farm did when we bought it. I tried to act nonchalant. "Nice car," I said.

He smiled. "It's the wife's," he said. "Mine is in the shop."

"Well," I said, "it's still nice."

He nodded as though the conversation wasn't as spiffy as he'd hoped it would be.

Or maybe it just seemed that way to me.

But no, my first assessment was probably correct. Because he glanced over at me and said, with a little note of irritation, "What, specifically, are your questions?"

"Oh, I don't know," I said. "I just sort of play it by ear."

As I said that, we came to a traffic light. I looked up to see a billboard bearing Santa's face smiling down on Standish and me.

It was Nicholas's brother; it had to be. It looked just like Nicholas. "I know his brother," I said. "I sat next to him on the plane. He looks just like that, only without a beard."

He ignored this brush with fame. "You seem familiar somehow," he said. "Could we have met?"

"Oh, I doubt it," I said. "I'm not from here."

"Few are," he said, pursing his too-pink lips and drumming on the steering wheel. When the light changed, he hit the gas so hard that I thought we'd both get whiplash.

"Well, okay," I said. "I'm from Texas."

Was it my imagination, or had we swerved a little when I'd said that?

" 'Texas,' " he repeated, turning to stare directly at me, even though we were on a ramp now, entering a freeway.

I stared back, even though, deep in my heart, I wanted at least one of us to be looking at the road.

Finally he went back to driving, but the expression on his face was tight and worried.

Ha! I thought. "So I don't see how we could have met," I told him. "Unless you have ties to Texas."

He cleared his throat. I could practically hear the wheels inside his head turning. Did he know, at this point, that we were playing cat and mouse? Or did he think the Texas reference was a coincidence?

I sat congratulating myself on my investigative technique.

"Your first trip to California?" he asked.

"Yes."

"Well, then. You should do a little sight-seeing." He grinned when he said this, and whipped toward an upcoming exit ramp. And it was an evil grin, too, although you probably think I'm making that up.

And sure enough, the next thing I knew we were on Forest Lawn Drive—and listen, even I know what Forest Lawn is.

It's a cemetery.

And there it was up ahead. "Forest Lawn," he said, his lip still curving upward as if he were smiling, but his eyes kind of menacing. "Now then," he said. "We'll go on to see the stars."

Stars. I had the feeling he meant the kind that you see in cartoon strips when some character has been bashed really hard. Except that I really had no way of proving that, and, indeed, no way of convincing anyone but me.

He was a clever SOB, but I wasn't going to back down just because he'd driven me past a place of eternal rest. Unless there wasn't anything sinister about it. Maybe he thought of it as a tourist attraction or something. Like, I know people in Austin who take everyone who visits to the LBJ Library. I know others who take them to the Congress Avenue Bridge to see the bats. So maybe Forest Lawn was just Standish's thing.

I tried to decide whether or not to mention Boots

LaRue. The speed of the cars flanking us made me decide that I shouldn't. At least, not yet. But I was giving him a chance to tell the truth here, and what he did in response was crucial. So, "Do you know anyone in Texas?" I asked him.

His face reddened slightly. Remember mood rings? That's the kind of giveaway I was getting from that.

"No," he said. "Can't say that I do."

Well, okay. So now I knew he was lying. But so what?

Except that it did seem to me that, when the time was right, I could drop some really tough question on him out of the blue, and, if nothing else, his coloration would give him away. And, even if it wouldn't hold up in court or even in a police station, at least *I* would know.

I could picture me saying it: *Did* you fake Wickie's death and get your partner, Boots LaRue, to sell the horse all over again to some hapless woman out in Oklahoma? Followed by, *And*, oh, yeah. Did you know the horse killed this woman? That would shake him up.

Seconds later, the Los Angeles Equestrian Center—heralded by what looked like miles and miles of white-board fencing—came into view.

"Jeez," I said, realizing that I'd seen the place before in a thousand movies and videos. You'd see the fences, and then, on the sound track, there'd be a lot of whinnying. In fact, on television especially, horses do nothing but whinny.

But there it was.

I pretty near forgot the sleuthing that had brought me to California.

The Los Angeles Equestrian Center. Whew. A veritable horseperson's paradise.

The whole place was ringed by mountains, some incredibly steep, and all thinly veiled in what I guess was smog. You could hear the unceasing sound of freeway traffic, but it was background.

Foreground was the sound of, not just one but several farriers, putting shoes on one or another cross-tied equine stars.

There were long shed rows serving as show barns and polo barns, and catering to all sorts of interests. A United Nations of horsedom instead of the isolated little coteries I was used to.

For instance, off in the distance was a horse pulling someone in a sulky, while a saddle-bred worked in another of the many small riding enclosures.

There were trailers and huge horse vans—the kind with ramps along the side.

There were people riding past in western tack. In one of the outdoor arenas, an instructor seated in a golf cart was shouting at a girl going over a small hunter course.

And everything was immaculate. All over the place, you could see wheelbarrows and garden carts for keeping them that way. Some of the barns—I guessed that they were leased by various stables—even had bright and beautiful beds of flowers gracing them.

I considered making a fertilizer joke, but when I glanced at Standish, he wore a look of impatience.

"Who are the movie stars on your client list?" I asked, genuinely wondering now.

"Let's see how many you can recognize," he said.

We got out of the car and walked toward a little

clutch of shops housed in a big white-frame building with green trim. On the left was a tack store. And on the right, unmistakably, based on the aroma, was a restaurant.

My stomach growled audibly.

"Lunch," he said, "might be an excellent idea."

Lunch! When he'd reach for his credit cards and notice they were gone! I couldn't take a chance. And I did, after all, still have that twenty-dollar bill in my jeans.

"Great," I said, biting down on my lower lip. "My treat."

CHAPTER 11

There wasn't anything like this complex in Texas—at least nothing that had survived. I mean, attempts had been made at various huge indoor facilities to pull something like this off, but they'd always gone belly-up.

I'm thinking Houston, San Antonio.

Maybe this one thrived because boarding seemed to be at the heart of it, whereas our attempts back home were always centered around shows.

And shows, period, with most folks opting to keep their horses at home or at a teeny stable somewhere. I guess in L.A., there isn't any space to do that.

This complex, Standish told me, had various entrepreneurs manning different sections of it—you know, a trainer with a dressage focus, or a reining focus, or a hunter-jumper person who took in boarders, gave lessons, et cetera.

"It used to be Griffith Park," he said. "They still call it that on some of the maps—'Griffith Park Equestrian Center'—although I haven't heard it called that by anyone. Sometimes people say 'Burbank Horse Center,' though." He went on to say that various big studios—Disney, Warner Bros., Universal—were right down the street, hence the place's appearance in a wealth of movies and TV shows.

"And your own movie star clientele," I reminded him.

"Let's just see if anyone is riding right now," he said. "I mean, before we stop for lunch."

I was so starstruck that I agreed, which, if you know me at all would be starstruck in the extreme. Because I do love to eat, and the airline's meager offering had long since been digested.

We walked into the area where there was an enormous, bleacher-surrounded indoor ring. EQUIDOME, the sign said. There were flags from a bunch of different nations—hey, don't get mad, I'm not a well-traveled person—hanging down from the massive roof.

Beyond the bleachers, Standish said, were two more dressage arenas and a large outdoor ring. What a place!

I could only say things like, "Wow," and "Gosh," I have to admit. A real rube.

"Oh, look," he said. "There's Cabrina Seton."

"Who?"

"Cabrina Seton," he said. "A starlet."

Said starlet was jiggling all over a put-upon looking palomino. She had plenty to jiggle, too. But she had that California waistline. You know, the kind you could circle with the thumb and forefinger of both your hands.

But there was no time to be tacky. Off in the distance I heard an unmistakable voice. "Oh, listen," I said, running off toward it. "I think that's Hilda Gurney!"

"Who?" he asked.

I turned to stare at him. I mean, how could an equine vet not know who Hilda Gurney was?

He glanced at his watch. "If we're going to have lunch," he said, "I suppose we ought to do it now."

But I had spotted—yes!—Sherry Sorum in the distance doing piaffe. "Look!" I said. "It's Sherry Sorum! And she's on one of her Andalusians, too."

He tried to guide my vision elsewhere. "There's Amanda Bonheur," he said, pointing at another zaftig lass.

"Who?"

"Amanda Bonheur. She was in . . . Oh, I can't remember the name of the movie, but the one with the three stewardesses that just came out," he said.

As if I'd go to see something about three stewardesses.

"Uh-huh," I said, about as politely as I could. "But I'd rather see Hilda Gurney and Sherry Sorum."

"Oh"—he looked disgustedly at me and then at his watch again—"we might as well eat."

Can you believe that I *reluctantly* followed him?

And Hilda Gurney and Sherry Sorum's illustrious presences were only partially responsible for my attitude. The other part was money—my lack thereof. Because the restaurant looked pretty posh. Like if they had anything so lowly as a burger, it would be a ten-dollar burger. Know what I mean?

There was a lot of glass and a lot of varnished oak. And a humongous oil painting of Rodney Jenkins going over a jump.

Oh, all those crisp white tablecloths and carefully folded cloth napkins! Things did not look good. I mean, the restaurant looked good. What did not look good were my chances of being able to pay for my meal and Ornell Standish's, too.

But I couldn't have him making the discovery that his cards were missing, now could I? Especially since he darn well knew that I had used the rest room at his clinic. Or, if he didn't know, he'd ask Miss Clemson and find out pretty quick.

Plus I'd offered to treat him. Which was about the equivalent of offering to replace Wickie for Louanne. God. Sometimes I wish I could keep my big mouth shut.

So there I was, surrounded by what were probably enormously expensive plates of crisp green salads and mile-high club sandwiches. There I was, ordering soup.

And there he was, debating whether the roast beef would win out over the provolone, chicken, and avocado.

That was probably why I popped up with, "So why and when exactly did you leave Texas?" Remember, he had kind of denied knowing anyone there.

His red-ringed eyes narrowed and he sat up taller in his chair. I thought of a cobra lifting itself out of a charmer's basket. A big fat cobra spreading its hood.

"Was it," I continued, "after Louanne Perry's horse allegedly died?"

He flushed.

"I knew you looked familiar," he said.

"Was it?" I persisted. "After Wickie allegedly—"

"Allegedly?" he asked, interrupting.

Well, there. I'd said it.

"Now I know exactly where I've seen you," he

said, pointing a pudgy, beringed finger across the table at me. "You're the one who . . . " And he leaned back, slapped the table, and laughed at me.

"Let me tell you something," I said. My dander was really up. I mean, who wants to be laughed at? "The horse who died that day wound up killing a woman out in Oklahoma not so very long ago."

I watched his eyes get bigger, and then I went on. "That's right. And now a friend of mine, Lola Albright, has the horse who, for all we know, might end up taking a run at her, too. So that's what you're responsible for," I said.

He looked amused. "Oh, I get it," he said. "You're the avenging angel."

You're the one, I wanted to say. The demonically cherubic one. And then I knew who he reminded me of: Rush Limbaugh. God, they could have passed for brothers. Twins. Ha! Which, I wondered, would be considered the evil twin?

I know. I sound hysterical. Still, I kept my voice as calm as I could. "I don't know why you did all this," I said, "but a lot of people have been hurt in the process."

He was shaking his head no, no, no. Was he going to deny everything? And where would that leave me? What had I gotten into here? Had I made a trip out here only to make a colossal fool of myself or what?

"The woman in Oklahoma," he said, "was a dingbat. Just like your friend Louanne Perry."

Aha!

"But you encouraged Louanne to buy the horse. For all I know, you encouraged the woman in Oklahoma, too."

"Louanne wanted to spend her money. The other

woman—I believe her name is Daisy, by the way—was in a similar frame of mind." He lowered his voice to a whisper. "A lot of people like to spend their money," he said. "It makes them feel very good."

"Well, what do you do?" I asked. "Just keep selling the same horse over and over?"

He stood up. "I have to make a phone call," he said.

He had a phone in his car. For a minute, I thought he'd go out to use it. But no. He walked to a Pacific Bell phone booth that was within my line of sight. Would he go to his wallet now and look for the credit cards? No. I watched as he punched in a gazillion numbers that he knew by heart.

Was he calling Boots LaRue?

Meanwhile his sandwich and my soup came.

I could smell the provolone.

He was gesticulating out there like crazy. Obviously in a state that would diminish his hunger, right?

So I lifted up a slice of his bread and moved the chicken aside, popping the provolone into my mouth.

Yummy.

I waited and watched and downed another piece of cheese while he went on talking. Needless to say, when he got off the phone and came back to the table, his sandwich was sans provolone. In fact, the avocado was, by this time, in short supply. I'd even eaten a couple of his chips.

But he was too furious to notice. He picked up what remained of the sandwich and chewed, talking, as you might imagine, at the same time. "So this friend of yours, she's the one who runs LoCo Farms?"

"Lola Albright," I said pointedly. "She's my best friend. Not to mention my next-door neighbor."

He smiled. A triumphant smile. I wanted to hit him in his big fat face with a key lime pie.

"Lola Albright," he said. And then he proceeded to describe her place. The stand of yucca at the entrance to the property. The curves in the drive. The way the outside of the house looked. The way you could see the horses in the background.

It was a threat. And you could even have had what he said on tape and never make anyone believe it was a threat, because it was only a description of where Lola and Cody lived. Except that he was telling me that he could find out anything he needed to know. That he was a man to be reckoned with.

"Did you drive past Forest Lawn to scare me?" I asked.

"Huh?"

Maybe not.

"Wickingham is alive, isn't he," I said. Not with any question mark at the end, either. "What do you and Boots LaRue do? Sell the same horse over and over?"

He flushed.

I was right, I thought.

"Whose idea was it?" I continued. "Yours or Boots's? And how many times has the horse been sold?"

Something flickered across Standish's fat face. I'd made some kind of error, but what? Something that made him realize that I really didn't know what I was talking about. So I segued back to what he'd said about Lola. About knowing where she lived and all. "And as far as Lola Albright goes," I said, "you just try it."

"Try it?" he said, all innocence. "Try what?"

The waitress arrived with the check. Standish leaned back so expertly that the server knew, intuitively, that I was to receive it. So *plop*—it was placed right in front of me, and then she walked away.

The total was twenty-six dollars. Six more than I had.

So what could I do?

I couldn't whip the credit card out, because the staff here probably knew Standish. And anyway, he might see. On the other hand, I couldn't even offer a check because my checkbook was back at the airport in my fanny pack.

Oy.

I called the waitress over.

"You'll have to deduct the soup," I said, gesturing at what, really, was a pretty full bowl.

She scowled. "Was something wrong with it?" she asked.

"I, uh . . . "

Then Standish leaned over and spoke to her. "You know," he said, "to be honest, there was barely anything in my sandwich. So maybe you ought to deduct that, too."

Now it was her turn. "I, uh . . . " she said. Then, "Well, okay." She wrote something across the check. "And I'm awfully sorry, Dr. Standish."

Whew.

* * *

I didn't know where this left us vis-à-vis the rest of the afternoon, but I didn't much care. I would be flying back to Texas in about three hours—and I had the satisfaction, at least, of knowing I'd been right about Wickingham. And I didn't really think Standish would make good on his threat to Lola. I mean, why would he? Still, just to make sure, I said, "Look. None of this will go any further. I just needed to know."

"Know what?"

"Stop playing stupid. I know that I didn't kill Wickie. That he didn't get colic and die while I was watching him."

"You are so very right," he said. "None of this will be going any further."

And he and I sort of stared each other down.

I think he'd have won, but one of his starlet chums came up to us. She was flashing her teeth and her jewelry and her cleavage. It provided ample distraction for the good doc.

"I, uh, well, uh . . . " I said, backing away and waving feebly. I scooted off and into the saddlery store as quickly as I could. I grabbed up several pairs of breeches and asked where the fitting room was.

Then I closed myself inside and waited.

But damn! I heard the door to the shop swing open; the clerk greeted Standish by name. Damn! I had managed to trap myself but good.

"Something I can help you with?" the clerk asked him.

"Actually," Standish said, "I'm looking for a friend. She's got brown hair, cut in a sort of bob. And she's maybe fifteen, twenty pounds overweight. She's—"

"I'm right here," I said, opening the dressing-room

door and thrusting the pile of breeches onto the countertop. "These," I said, "are all too small." Then I gestured at him, at his too-tight white suit. "Kind of like yours," I said.

The clerk tittered, and, whatever my peril, I was momentarily gratified.

I ran outside like a shot.

CHAPTER 12

I turned away from the parking lot toward the arenas. I walked at a good clip, a pace that wouldn't seem like panic, but at the same time, would be tough for fat boy to maintain.

Wrong.

In fact, I could hear him maintaining it. Wheezily, to be sure. Well, let him. And I wasn't going to even so much as glance behind me to see how close he was.

I mean, what was he, a respected veterinarian, going to do right here, in the middle of bunches of people, and in broad daylight, too? Except that I didn't like the fact that he kept on coming. Because that meant that he had something in mind.

And, the truth be told, we had reached a section where there weren't any people. Only horses. Horses peering out of their half-door stalls at him and me.

And he must have noticed it, too, because he came running up behind me. I felt his pudgy fingers on my shoulders and then, almost immediately, on my neck.

And I thought of my old gym teacher, Miss Barr. My old gym teacher, who was convinced that every single girl in her charge would one day be mayhemed. My old gym teacher, whose favorite sport was self-defense.

I stooped, and Standish, pushed by his own momentum, went catapulting over my shoulder.

Trouble was, I fell with him. And as we were both getting up, he started rolling my way, his arms reaching out in my direction.

A button flew off his suit and *ping*ed my cheek. "Ow," I said, leaping to my feet and running.

I saw some cowboys in the distance waving at me. Well, I guessed they were cowboys, although their outfits looked awfully garish and way too clean.

"Help!" I shouted, and they looked my way, but didn't make a move in my direction. "Help!"

One of them held his hand up and made a thumbs-up sign with it. The others mimicked applause.

And Standish was right behind me, his big hand reaching out.

"Help," I said, more shrilly than before.

Standish bulldozed into me, and I fell. He dropped on top of me, knocking the breath from my body so that I could only look up at him, gasping, and hoping that my bones would hold up.

His face was red and sweat was rolling from his forehead and dripping down into his eyes. He rubbed at them—and sputtered some approximation of a laugh.

"They . . . (breath) . . . think . . . (breath) . . . this . . . is . . . a . . . (breath) . . . movie," he gasped. "I . . . can . . . kill . . . you . . . right . . . "

I reached up, and, disgusting as it sounds, jammed my finger inside his right nostril. I pushed as hard as I could. "Yeah," I said, as he peeled his body off mine.

"What's the name of the flick?" A cowboy shouted.

"The Life and Times of Miss Barr," I called back as I got to my feet and started running again. She had told us to use any means available when faced with a male assailant. Male assailants, indeed, had been Miss Barr's worst—although probably unrealized—fear.

Off against the fence line was a little buckskin horse. He was decked out in a silver-laden western saddle and his bridle reins were on the ground.

I beelined toward him, ready to vault on if I had to. But I didn't have to. He turned to watch my approach, then, just before I got to a place where I could mount, he dipped into a camellike bow to make the process easier.

I grabbed the reins and swung up into the saddle, banging my pubic bone on that great big horn that western saddles have.

"Hey, that's the marshal's horse," I heard someone holler.

"This ain't no movie!" another voice said. It was one of the cowboys. He'd figured it out far too late to benefit me.

Standish grabbed for my leg, but he was too late. I was galloping off, and behind me—not just Standish but a lot of people—were shouting, "Hey! Hey! Hey!"

I turned toward a big open field and fortunately stopped when I saw the sign. DO NOT ENTER, it read. HIGH-PRESSURE SPRINKLERS COULD ACTIVATE AT ANY TIME. Now *that* would be charming. Especially since there was a huge Irish bank for horses to jump—two tiers—in there. I could just see my little buckskin leaping it, impaling me on the saddle as the high-pressure sprinklers activated.

But where to go?

There was a perimeter trail; I could see people on it, but Standish would probably figure I'd gone that way. Besides, it was wide enough for him to drive on, so that catching me wouldn't be any problem. And as I now realized, he really could do anything at all to me in broad daylight and everyone around here would assume it was a film.

No cameras? No problem. They'd think it was a rehearsal.

But meanwhile, what to do? All the while I was pondering, I was really moving out, but I couldn't go far at that pace. Oh, not that the little buckskin wasn't enjoying the ride, but I was out the main gate all too quickly and then on concrete.

So, even though my life appeared to be depending on it, I didn't want to gallop madly off, maybe ruining this game little horse for life.

So I walked up the sidewalk past the gleaming stucco condos called the Parkside Equestrian Estates, then by an older building based on the same theme. This was a building called the Royal Equestrian.

Several young blond men came out and pointed at me. "That's the marshal's horse," one of them squealed.

Great. I had to be riding a celebrity horse.

So, like it or not, I picked up a trot and began cutting between buildings, zigging and zagging.

I zigged and zagged past men in Avantis and Mercedes and what seemed a hundred girls driving Jeeps. And then there I was, at Walt Disney Studios.

I know what you're thinking. You're thinking that eventually I would end up mingling with the likes of Donald Duck and Mickey Mouse, and Goofy aren't you?

But that was not to be. I just kept on going until I was in an older, shabbier part of town, where I turned into the lot of a little pizza place that appeared to have gone out of business and hid between the Dumpster and a huge vine-encrusted, wrought-iron fence.

And it turned out to be the right choice, too. Because sirens were going off everywhere, as if there had been some massive jailbreak—and the master criminal who was now on the loose was yours truly.

But now what?

As if in response, the horse gave a great big rasperry, coating me with snot.

I realized at this point that I stood a far better chance of getting away if I weren't accompanied by a horse, but I didn't see any way out of it. At least not now. Except that I had to somehow get back to the airport, and I didn't think a taxi would stop for us both.

Unless . . .

I saw a pickup coming down the street, a long stock trailer in tow. I pulled the reins over the buckskin's head and let them hit the ground, pretty certain that he'd stay. I mean, I'd seen Western horses ground tied that way and that's how he'd been standing when I'd stolen him, right?

So I ran out and toward the truck, my arms waving frantically.

The driver—one of the garnishly dressed cowboys, it seemed—stopped.

"My horse," I said, "he's just exhausted. Could you. . . ?" I gestured at the empty trailer.

It *was* one of the cowboys, because he said, "I saw your scene. It was fabulous." I guess he wasn't the one who had figured things out.

"Thanks. But my horse . . . " I made a sweeping arm movement in the direction of the Dumpster.

"He's not hurt, is he?"

"Nope," I said, thinking that maybe he wasn't even back there anymore. That maybe he had wandered off. Where he'd doubtless be mugged for his saddle. "Wait right here."

I rounded the Dumpster and—what a good boy!—there he was. I led him forward, smiling until I saw the look of incredulity on the cowboy's face.

"Hey!" he shouted. "That's *my* horse!"

"You're the marshal?" I asked. Well, great. Because maybe he could get me back to catch my plane safely. "Could you arrest someone and take me to the airport?" I asked. "Or maybe take me to the airport first."

"You steal my horse and you want me to take you to the airport?"

"You're a marshal," I whined.

"I'm the *parade* marshal," he said. "I'm the head of the Gay Rodeo Association and I lead the rodeo parade. And we're supposed to be rehearsing right now, too." He looked miffed.

"Well, okay," I said. "But you could still take me to the airport."

"I'm taking you to jail," he said, stepping toward me.

So I left the buckskin there and ran, figuring that the cowboy wouldn't waste his time in hot pursuit. I mean, he'd load his horse and then he'd go someplace and report me, right? And get on with his parade rehearsal, yes?

Wrong.

And this was no Ornell Standish. This was a young, lithe, and extremely speedy cowboy.

He'd have had me, too, if the horse hadn't whinnied kind of excitedly, causing both the cowboy and me to turn around and look to see what was up.

And what was up was a couple of teenagers, one already behind the wheel of the cowboy's rig and another trying to get the buckskin into the trailer.

The cowboy shook his fist at me. "You set up a diversion," he accused. "Well, you won't get away with it," he yelled. He was already rushing back to his horse's aid and shouting at me over his shoulder. "I'll see that all three of you end up in jail."

Jail. It sounded so safe.

Despite being rattled, I walked slowly now, catching my breath and trying to formulate something like a plan. In the distance, I could still hear sirens, so the cops and probably Standish, too, were out there trolling for me.

What was I to do?

I spied a dry cleaning shop and thought that maybe, just maybe, part of my troubles were over.

Because I've gotten dry cleaning out a bunch of times without my ticket, haven't you?

A smiling Oriental man bobbed up to the counter.

"Washington," I said. "I forgot my ticket."

"Washington," he said, trundling off into the recesses of the shop.

He held up a plastic bag with several garments in it. "Washington," he said.

I squinted at it. It kind of looked too big, but hey. I pulled the twenty dollars out of my pocket and thanked him.

But twenty dollars wasn't enough.

"I don't have any more," I said. And then, "I'll tell you what." I lifted the plastic shield and began going through the garments, yanking out a hideously beaded pink dress. "I'll just take this," I said.

I was tempted to run out without my change, but I didn't want to seem any more suspicious than I already did.

He came back with a five.

"Fifteen dollars!" I said.

"The beads," he explained.

I glared at him and left, walking half a block before crouching behind a stand of gorgeous bougainvillea to change.

Okay, I'm at the airport, having walked. I still had my jeans and top, but I didn't dare do anything but carry them folded. I figured the police would have an APB out for someone dressed as I had *been* dressed, so this dress was perfect.

But I was going to end up in one of those *Glamour* magazine Don't! spreads, I could tell.

Because all through my walk, and it was probably three miles or so, and it took me over an hour, people kept staring at me and kind of moving away. I mean, the dress wasn't disreputable or anything. I mean, if it were, why have it cleaned? It was the fit, maybe, about six sizes too large, and the high-topped tennies I was wearing with it, I suppose. Because it was a pretty dressy dress. If you know what I mean. Of course, if Julia Roberts were wearing it, it would become next month's fad, but a Julia Roberts, as you've probably deduced by now, I'm not.

Anyway, I walked vigorously, swinging whichever arm wasn't carrying my real clothes. I kept imagining Covert Bailey of *Fit or Fat* fame smiling down at me from above as I made each stride, but it didn't help me enjoy it. Because, at any moment, a swarm of police cars, or worse, Ornell Standish, could materialize beside me, right? Not to mention an irate urban cowboy *and* his horse.

But eventually I came to it: the airport.

But my spirits lifted when, maybe ten minutes later, a friendly-faced man in a guard's uniform walked toward me, fanny pack in hand. He handed it to me, and I looked inside.

"We have a form we'd like you to sign," he said.

I wondered how I ought to do it. As Orlando Washington? Or as myself?

But then he solved the problem. "Miz Vaughan?" he asked, as if I hadn't heard him.

"Of course." I reached for the form and the ballpoint and scrawled. *Boy,* I thought. *The airlines really don't give a hoot about people using phony names. I wonder why they ask for names in the first place?*

Then, at the man's direction, I opened the bag.

My wallet, with the cash I'd had in it, was gone. So was my return ticket. I guess my gasp told him as much.

"I'm sorry," he said.

What *was* in there was my Texas driver's license and my United States Dressage Federation membership card. So great. At least I didn't have to spend an hour or more getting a new driver's license. And I didn't have any credit cards.

Of my own, I mean.

"Count your blessings," the man said. "And Merry Christmas."

"Merry Christmas," I said.

But the fact was, the Christmas spirit was probably what made the thief leave anything at all.

And, of course, it was a she. I'd left the bag in the ladies' room, hadn't I?

Christmas.

Its proximity, the ticket clerk delighted in telling me, meant that I wouldn't be able to change my ticket—which, by the way, was going to cost more than two hundred dollars over what I'd paid to travel as Orlando Washington.

"Unless . . . " the agent said, and left it there.

"Unless what?"

"Unless you want to go standby," she said.

Standby. "What does that mean?" I asked.

She laughed uncomfortably.

Okay, I wanted to say, *so I'm not a world traveler. So disembowel me.*

I handed her one of Ornell Standish's credit cards and held my breath while she explained that I could be out on the next flight—or have to wait until maybe Christmas Day. "But all it will take in your case is one no-show. That shouldn't take too long. Sometimes we have whole families going standby and that's tough. Thank you, Miss Standish," she said, handing the card back to me.

Whew. Or nearly so. Because Nicholas—you remember him—turned out to be standing right behind me, and he was saying, "Ah, Miss *Standish*.

I'd been led to believe it was Miss Washington. Or should I say Miss Vaughan."

I stared at him. After all I'd been through, he was the least of my worries. I didn't owe him even part of an explanation, I decided. I turned on my heel and began to walk away.

"Just a moment," he said, catching hold of my shoulder.

I winced, because my shoulder had taken a lot of abuse.

But then he was flashing his wallet—and the overhead light caught and twinkled over something that looked like a badge. "Drug Enforcement Administration," he said. "Follow me through those doors over there."

I am seated in a gray metal chair at a gray metal table, and Nicholas is whining. "What am I supposed to believe? You tell me your name is one thing, then another, and now you have a third name and—"

"See here," I said. "You were invited to come along with me. Instead you left."

"Because I believed you. I figured nobody could invent a story as boring as the one you told. But I have since learned . . . "

"Learned what?"

"Yeah, well . . . boring me to death was a pretty good technique. But later, when I found out you'd left your fanny pack in some drop site—"

"I left it in the bathroom! It was an accident!"

He and I glared at each other. "Prove it," he said, crossing his arms.

I took a deep breath. I mean, how do you prove that you weren't transporting heroin or cocaine—

street value fifty million dollars? And anyway, wasn't *he* supposed to be proving that I was? I mean, isn't that the way it's supposed to work?

Except that I set about doing it anyway. I unstrapped my fanny pack and waved it in his face. "What was I carrying? How could I fit it in here? Unless it was a microdot or something—you know, like corporate espionage stuff. Maybe it wasn't drugs at all."

He looked uncomfortable.

"You had that packet I gave you analyzed, didn't you?" I said accusingly.

He looked even more uncomfortable.

"Ha! What did you think it was? High-grade heroin or something? Ha!" I was about to launch into a tirade about my tax dollars.

He snatched the fanny pack away from me and shook it. "I don't know . . . " he said.

"And how could I know that the pickup person was going to go to the bathroom after me, huh?"

"That's nothing," he said. "That kind of thing—drop, pickup—happens all the time."

"Whatever. But how. . . ?" And then my eyes started widening as an idea dawned. "Hey," I said. "My return ticket was in that bag. So whoever picked it up is probably in the waiting room right now. Expecting to board a flight to Austin at three-fifteen."

"As Orlando Washington," he said.

"Right."

"Okay," he said. "I'll try that." And he reached under the metal table and tried pressing something, although eventually he had to bend down and peer under there to be able to hit it.

Sure enough, another man was thus summoned. They conferred; the other man left.

"So?" I asked.

Nicholas sat down and shrugged. "So we'll see."

"Well, listen," I said, "can I make a couple of phone calls while we're waiting?"

"What kind of phone calls?" he asked.

"To the credit card companies."

"Oh," he said. "Are you contending that you had credit cards in your bag?"

"No. I told you about taking Standish's cards, didn't I? Well, anyway . . . I took his cards and I want to call—"

He waved his hand in a way that shut me up. "No. Look," he said, "I halfway believe you. And it's none of my business what you took from the good doctor so long as it wasn't drugs. But really, I can't have you making calls about these credit cards from here. Not with me sitting here."

"You could leave." I tried.

"Forget it." Then he looked at me, in my pink beaded dress. "There is one thing you *can* do, though. I'm assuming you'd want to."

"And that is?"

"Change clothes."

Just as I was coming out of the little room where I'd gotten back into my jeans, the door opened—and the man Nicholas had summoned ushered in a woman who, had she been younger, would have been called a waif.

She was maybe sixty, and wearing, I guess, everything she owned. A layered look, but definitely low fashion, with everything *really*—as opposed to artfully—mismatched.

Her eyes traveled over me and then landed on my fanny pack.

She became instantly terrified. Her lower lip was trembling and so were her hands. "I found it," she was babbling. "I thought it was the Lord's way of telling me what he wanted me to do. A gift from his angels," she said.

Nicholas hammered at her anyway. "Think," he commanded her. "What was in that bag?"

She told him—right down to the three cellophane-wrapped Lemonheads, which, alas, she admitted to having eaten. "Et," was what she said.

Well, they *are* pretty good if you like things tart.

"Anything else?" Nicholas demanded.

"I left her driver's license," the woman said. "And some kind of card that looked official."

"My USDF card," I said. "It's a dressage thing."

Nicholas rolled his eyes. "Enough," he said, his chair scraping as he stood. "Both of you can go."

"Wait," I said. "Is that your brother on the Santa billboards? I mean, really?"

"You betcha," he said.

"Listen," I said to the woman once we were out of that room, "I would really like to have my ticket back. But listen, you can have *my* ticket in return. See? Then I can get home when I said I would, and you can come to Austin next time there's an available seat."

She looked unconvinced.

"Look," I said, "that ticket really is mine."

"Except," she answered, "it wasn't written in the same name as the driver's license was. It said—"

"I know what it said." I interrupted her. "But the

point is, I paid cash for that ticket. So whatever name it says, it's mine."

She looked as though she was processing that.

"What name's your other ticket in?" she asked.

"Ornell Standish," I told her.

"Ornell." She weighed it. "Seems like a better name for a woman than Orlando."

"Definitely," I told her.

"And I can stay here at the airport until there's room?"

"Yes." I hoped that was true. But it probably was. I mean, she was a ticketed passenger.

"Or you could sell the ticket. For money."

"Cash?" she asked.

"Sure. So either way, you make out."

I waited. Hoped. Prayed.

They were calling the flight, too. "Look," I said, "I'll throw this in." I unfurled the pink beaded dress.

"Oooh," she said, standing back to admire it. Then she decided. "Okay," she said, grabbing the dress as if she feared I'd change my mind. Then she gave me her ticket, and I gave her mine.

Shortly afterward I was in Phoenix with an hour to kill. I took Standish's credit cards and made the calls that Nicholas, in Burbank, wouldn't let me make. And it wasn't as simple as punching in numbers; I actually had to talk to a person, but it worked out okay. I said I was who I am, Robin Vaughan, and that I was calling for Dr. Standish. As soon as they heard "Doctor Standish," they accepted that someone else would be making the calls. And after all, I had all the information: the number of the credit card; even, as it turned out, the correct zip.

What I found out was, although the good doctor hadn't charged a ticket to Houston, which might have connected him to LaRue, he'd done better than that: He'd charged one to Oklahoma City.

Making a house call, perhaps, to a woman named Daisy. A fatal house call.

CHAPTER 13

It was after nine when the plane landed in Austin. Cody was in the terminal waiting for me. “Hurry up,” he said. “The puppy’s out in the car alone.”

So big deal, I thought. It was nighttime, and it wasn’t very hot. I mean, when it’s hot, you really can’t leave animals in cars. But now?

“He’s very dependent,” Cody explained. “I almost tried to smuggle him in with me.”

Oh, great. I needed to get picked up and questioned for consorting with a dog smuggler, yet.

But when we got to the car, I saw what he meant. The dog was lying in a heap as though, without Cody, life was pointless and not worth living. “Aw.” I picked the puppy up, but he wriggled free. Cody was all he was interested in.

“Hmm,” I said. “This is going to be a great present for Jeet.”

Cody laughed weakly. “So what happened?” he asked me.

I found myself telling him about Standish’s trip to Oklahoma. I was almost afraid to ask what he thought. But I had to know. Did he think Standish could actually have killed his friend’s wife, then let the horse take the rap for it?

"Well," Cody said, "My chum did say that Daisy threatened LaRue with a lawsuit. I guess the two of them figured that if she sued, their whole scam would come out."

"Except what scam could that be? I mean, LaRue is a high-rolling horse dealer and Standish is a vet. I mean, they don't need to make money selling and reselling the same horse."

Cody was shaking his head in agreement. "And especially that horse. Because he is definitely a charger," he said. "I mean, big time." He described Lo's one and only encounter with him in the field. It had taken place in my absence. "It made my heart stand still," Cody said. "If Lola hadn't held her ground . . ."

"But still. That doesn't mean the horse killed poor Daisy."

Cody thought about it. "I don't know," he said.

"Well, could you call your friend?" I asked. "I mean as soon as we get back. Ask him exactly how it happened. Because he didn't charge Lola out in the paddock, remember? So Daisy would have had to stand out in the middle of a pasture or something—and then probably, she'd have had to run when the horse came at her. Otherwise, he'd have backed off the way he did when Lola just stood there," I said.

"Yeah," Cody said, "but it takes guts to stand. Believe me, I'd have thought about running."

I smiled, picturing Lo. She had guts, all right. Cody was smiling, too. In admiration, both of us.

"Okay," Cody said. "I'll call. When we get in, write down exactly what you want to know."

"Well, you might not want to do this when you

hear," I said, thinking that he, like my vet, might find some of the questions a tad too direct.

Did Dix know Dr. Ornell Standish?

"Okay," Cody said.

"And . . ." I paused.

"Come on," Cody said. "Spit it out."

"Okay," I said. "Did the man actually see the horse kill his wife? And how big was the enclosure where his wife's body was found? And what day, exactly, was that?"

"You're right," Cody said. "I can't ask him stuff like that. I'll tell him you're Lola and you have a couple of things you want to know. Then *you* can ask him. Maybe he'll think it's related to the horse's retraining or something."

"That'll work," I said.

"Except Lola will kill me, because she'd never in a million years ask anybody rude stuff like that."

Rude, rude. What is this obsession with rude? I mean, how else can you find out what you need to know without a single conversation taking a hundred and fifty years?

Besides, it wasn't as though I didn't think that Cody's friend wasn't still very broken up about poor Daisy. It was just that this was necessary info.

"Stop with the explanations," Cody said. We were walking through the front door now. "Let's just do it."

The thing was, the friend was not, in fact, reticent at all. Or he didn't let on that he was still upset. He said no, he'd never heard of Standish. No, he hadn't actually seen the murder—that was what he called it—by the horse. And the horse was in its pen as it usually was.

"How big was the pen?" I asked.

He cited dimensions that roughly jibed with the paddock dimensions at Lo's.

"But I thought the horse didn't charge if he was in a paddock. I thought he only did it out in the pasture," I persisted.

Cody listened to my end with an expression of disapproval on his face. I think the puppy was attempting the same look.

"He used to only do it when he was out in the field," the man said patiently. "But that day, he did it in the pen."

"But you didn't actually see . . . "

"I saw the result," he said. "And now, if you don't mind, I'd really like not to talk about this anymore."

"Okay, but what was the date?"

"I'll tell you," he said, "but then I would very much like to get off the phone."

Fair enough.

When I hung up, I said, "Cody, I think Standish did poor Daisy in."

"Flying to Oklahoma doesn't mean anything. It isn't proof."

"On the same day that the woman was killed?"

"Even on the same day. I mean, come on. Look at the O. J. thing. All *they* had."

"No," I said. "Standish did it. I know he did, because why else would he have tried to kill me?"

"He *what*?"

I guess I'd neglected to mention it. I gave Cody the details of my narrow escape at the Los Angeles Equestrian Center.

For once, he didn't scoff. "Aw, shit. We'd better go to the sheriff."

"But where does that leave Lola?" I asked, thinking she'd have to return the horse.

"Oh my God," he said.

"What?"

"If Standish called somebody from the restaurant, maybe he's going to come steal the horse. Get rid of the evidence, sort of. I mean, he came back and seemed to know who she was. You said he described LoCo Farms and everything."

"If anything, he'd come back to kill Lola," I said.

"Robin," Cody said, "chill out. You're beginning to sound like some kind of nut. And you've got me sounding like one. The fact is, the business in California was probably the end of it."

I was going to argue, but I realized that would only make things worse.

"Here," Cody said, pushing the puppy toward me. "Rub a puppy. It'll help calm you down."

"That's right," I said. "He couldn't be coming to get Lola because he couldn't have gotten a flight. But where is she?"

"Shopping," Cody said. "She'll be home any minute."

"I don't know . . ." I said.

"Robin, the guy may have been ticked off while you were there, but trust me. Now that you're here, this whole thing's probably over. I mean, the guy is not going to risk—"

"You're right," I said. "I'm tired. I'm talking crazy. I should just go to my place, then. Make sure Teresa has been holding down the fort, feeding the animals, et cetera."

"I'll drive you."

"No," I said. "I'll walk. It'll clear my head, I think." Plus my joints felt as though they needed a lube.

"Check the barn," he said. "Make sure Noel is in his stall and not out in the field."

"So what are you guys doing? Never turning him out?"

"No. Lola's going to turn him out all by his lonesome. Soon as she gets in."

"So what makes you think he could be out now?"

"Nothing makes me think it," Cody said, with irritation. "I was just being cautious. But what the hell. Go on out without checking. Get yourself trampled. See if I care."

Jeez.

I entered the barn without switching on the light and listened—and felt better, calmer, right away. Because you know what it's like. The steady chomp, chomp, chomp of horses eating away. The occasional skitter of a mouse. A little thud as a horse hits a shoe up against the wall or something.

I walked down the row of stalls and spoke to each of the horses. Most of them were troublemakers Lo had taken into training. They eyed me warily, but most of them acknowledged my presence in some way.

Not Noel. I stood at his stall door and cooed at him, but he was evidently way, way in the corner eating his hay and totally ignoring me.

Well, that was fine. I was glad Lo had him, because she could deal with the vice that he'd learned. Anyone else would have gotten hurt, and then where would the horse end up? In an Alpo can, probably.

"You're a lucky boy," I told the darkness, and a reluctant nicker and a shift in his weight said he thought so, too.

* * *

I let myself into the pasture connecting LoCo Farms to our farm and walked on.

It was colder than usual, with the sky bright with stars and clear. I looked up, searching for constellations.

I've never been able to do that, identify the patterns that astronomers talk about, but I always try. I kept walking as I did so, though, because the land was open and I was pretty sure of the way.

I heard something crashing around far behind me. The puppy, I thought. I stood and waited, even calling, "Rooney, come on, boy," a couple of times to no avail before moving on. But it was a good sign—that he was at least contemplating leaving Cody and coming with me.

I was still wondering how to make a connection between Standish and LaRue, though. I hadn't, so far, been able to do that. Despite all that Standish had done, in the proof department, I was still nil.

I could go to Houston, I thought. And if LaRue, whom I'd never met, knew who I was, that would do it. If he'd heard anything at all about me, it would be clinched.

But it would be clinched for *me*. It wasn't exactly proof that would make a district attorney sit up and take notice.

Oh, God. I sometimes wonder why I get embroiled in weird situations all the time anyway.

Still, even if it just clinched things for me alone, it was something I needed to do. Then I could tell a D.A. everything, and if the D.A.'s office wanted to investigate, fine.

But would it be the Harris County D.A.—because that's where Houston was, or would it be the Los

Angeles County D.A.—because I thought that's where Burbank was? Or would it be Oklahoma, where Daisy had lived—or here, because of the horse thing?

Oy. In real life, nothing's ever simple.

On the other hand, maybe it is. Maybe all I had to do was call Boots LaRue and pretend I knew everything and he'd confess, like in Perry Mason. Or else steal LaRue's credit cards and try tracing what he'd charged. I mean, I'd had good luck with Standish's cards. Maybe he and LaRue had the same itinerary. You know, LaRue would turn out to be his accomplice in Daisy's murder. They'd have gone to Oklahoma together.

Yes.

But it would have to wait until morning, I thought, as I opened the wooden gate between our farms and prepared to slip onto my own property.

Except that right then I heard a yelp. A puppy yelp, I thought. And it came from somewhere behind me.

So the pup *had* followed after all, and now he was out there, lost.

The Macaroon.

My heart swelled as I closed the gate and made my way back the way I'd come. "Rooney," I called. "It's okay. It's okay, Rooney."

Then I stopped cold.

It was Rooney, all right, but it was Rooney tugging at the trousers of a man. I couldn't see who, but it wasn't Cody—he was way too fat.

In fact, it looked like Ornell Standish, but, of course, it couldn't be. And the man was trying to kick The Macaroon, who seemed to be enjoying the game.

But what should I do? I was wondering. Should I scream or run or what? I mean, a meter reader, this was not. Unless I was so tired, so out of it that I was hallucinating.

Was it Standish? Would he dare? And how could he be here? I mean, how? He would practically have had to have been on the same plane with me.

I came closer, but tentatively. On the assumption that, if I could see him, he could see me. But I knew the terrain and he didn't.

Plus, if it was Standish, where did he get off, trying to kick my husband's dog? Who, by the way, had gone from doing a pretty good cut and dodge to doing a *great* cut and dodge.

But then the dog, momentarily, stopped tussling and looked back toward Lola's. I did, too.

The big outdoor light beside Lola's barn went on.

And there was Noel, silhouetted in it. He'd been turned out at last, and he was observing us humans down below.

Standish—I could see him now—hadn't stopped to look back toward the hill. He kept advancing in my direction. I guess I should have been scared, but I wasn't. I was angry instead. Still, I knew I couldn't just let even a villain like Standish get mowed down by a horse.

"Watch out," I said. "The horse is out. Just hold your ground and you'll be fine."

"Ha!" he said. "Oldest trick in the book."

Behind him, Noel had picked up a trot.

"Are you deaf? Can't you hear those hoofbeats?" They sounded like timpani to me.

Standish cackled. "I don't think so," he said, pulling something out of his pocket.

But the horse was closer now. Close enough for me to see that his ears were laid back and his teeth were bare. It was a serious posture, and for a minute I thought of Lola—standing stock-still in the face of it—and hoped that I could approximate her daring.

Then *bam!* Noel exploded forward and was coming full bore ahead. At one of us, but which one?

"Just be still," I said, unsure how the horse would interpret Standish's forward movement.

Then Standish let out a shriek. It had nothing to do with the horse. It had to do with his own attack mode. It was like something he'd seen in an old kung fu movie.

He held the thing he'd pulled from his pocket high and came running at me, *whoop*ing. It would have been comical, this fat guy in a too-tight white suit rushing forward like that, but, because of what was in his hand, it wasn't.

It was a syringe, a big one.

"The horse!" I said, thinking more of running than of standing still. "Oh, Lola, Lola. You'd better be right." I closed my eyes and waited, wishing I could lift off like Mary Poppins or Commander Cody or even Mary Martin in *Peter Pan*, strings and all.

The thunder of the horse's hooves rose in volume, but only briefly. It was coupled with a muttered, "Oh, damn!" from Standish, and a sort of thick, sucking noise. The hoofbeats rolled past me; I opened my eyes to see Standish sprawled practically at my feet.

The horse tossed his head and kicked out, snorting. Then he came for another pass.

CHAPTER 14

You probably know by now that I'm not a very brave person.

Oh, I've had brave moments, but it's almost as though I'm not in charge of them. What I mean is, in the clinches, it's as if some braver me that lives way deep inside comes out and takes over.

Please. I'm not talking about having multiple personalities or anything like that. I just mean, when the real me wants to get out of Dodge, this other part won't let me go.

Like when I'm driving and some situation occurs that requires emergency action. Some macho part of me elbows the chicken part out of the way and does whatever needs to be done.

Or at least it feels that way.

So there I was, the real me, waiting for Miss Macho. And here was Noel, not realizing that Miss Macho hadn't arrived. It was odd, almost as if the visual part of it were being done in slo-mo. I could see the horse's big hindquarter muscles rippling, his long neck straining forward with every stride. It had an eerie kind of beauty. And the sound! His hoofbeats seemed amplified in the clear night air, *ba-da-dum, ba-da-dum, ba-da-dum.*

I kept thinking of the strangest things. That

Tennyson poem where you first learn about iambic tetrameter. The one that goes "*Half-a-League, Half-a-League.*" The one that also says, "*Into the Valley of Death . . .*"

I shook that thought away, and the very next thing that popped into my mind was that scene in the movie of *Under the Volcano*, where Albert Finney is staggering up that narrow path and the white horse gallops into him like a linebacker. I kept thinking of Katerina Schwetman, too. And above all, I kept thinking that I'd better hold my ground here or get pummeled the way Ornell Standish had just been.

Ornell Standish.

Boy, I was going to survive this if only to be able to bruit the truth about the man. What a slimeball! He'd not only feigned Wickie's death and had the horse resurface, but he'd killed the woman to whom the horse had eventually been resold. And now he'd come here to try to kill me. Again!

Just how had he expected to pull that off? I mean, didn't he think someone would be suspicious, me being found dead out in the middle of Lola's back pasture? Or had he been planning to bash me up a bit so that it looked as though Noel had done it?

Oh, it made me furious. So furious that, with Noel maybe two strides away, I not only didn't run, I stepped toward him, flapped out both hands, and said, "Haw," or something throaty like that.

Miss Macho *still* hadn't arrived, mind you. I'd just worked myself up with what I was thinking. And it was better than holding my ground—because Noel put on the brakes in that amazing way horses can and stopped maybe two feet in front of me.

His ears had been pinned back, but it was only an

act. The minute he stopped, his ears pricked forward again. And he took a cautious step toward me with this sort of dopey look on his face, like, Duh? Did I do something naughty?

Well. I guess you could count killing Ornell Standish as naughty, except that, at that moment, I didn't exactly feel that Standish had gotten something he didn't deserve.

Of course, I would still have to call 911, because they might be able to coax some life back into him. From where I stood, though, his sprawl looked final. So final that I considered reaching into his billfold to notify his next of kin.

The puppy made a beeline back toward Lola's, and I thought that maybe I should, too, except that I did have to make that emergency call—and I was closer to Primrose than to Loco Farms at this point.

The horse began nuzzling me, as if checking me out for treats. Still, I didn't dare *run* toward Primrose lest he think the game was on again.

Then two things happened simultaneously: Standish groaned; and Cody, from back in the direction of their place, called my name.

"Over here," I called out. But it scared me to, in effect, be alerting Standish as well as Cody to my whereabouts. I mean, true, Standish seemed pretty out of it, but still . . .

"You all right?" Cody's voice was closer now.

"Yeah."

Then Cody appeared. "I thought you were long gone. That's why I turned him out."

"I thought Lo was going to do that," I said, with more accusation in my voice than I'd planned.

"I thought I'd save her the trouble. I mean, it's late and she's not back yet, and . . . "

I glanced at Standish's body, wondering if he could have somehow gotten to Lo. But no, I didn't see how he could.

"Jesus," Cody said. "Who . . . ?" He was kneeling at Standish's side before I could answer the question. He had his hand at Standish's throat, taking his pulse, I think.

"That's Standish," I said. "Noel ran him over. I mean, Standish ran and then Noel . . . "

Cody stood up. "We've got to get an ambulance or something," he said. "This guy's out cold."

"Should we carry him to the farm or what?"

"I don't think so," Cody said. "I think . . . " He wasn't sure, and for some reason, I had nothing to contribute to help him. "I'll go call," he decided at last. "You wait here with him."

I didn't want to, but arguing seemed wrong. "Okay," I said.

I watched Cody disappear toward my place, the puppy scampering beside him as though he couldn't imagine anything that was more fun.

Noel strolled after them for a few paces, then turned and came back to remain with me. I stroked his neck, grateful for his presence as I stared down at the vanquished Standish. I felt my anger return. To my shame, I found myself thinking that poetic justice had been cheated by the fact that Standish was still alive.

He groaned again, and even moved.

The horse snorted as if in derision. "That's what I say," I agreed.

Then Standish was rolling onto his side and propping himself up on one of his elbows.

"We've called an ambulance," I said. Then I got an

idea. "But look . . . you're dying," I told him. "So why not confess to everything?"

He coughed. I actually think it was a laugh that he aborted at the last minute. He tried to get up, though.

"Stupid Oklahoma woman," he finally said, maybe three, four words at a time. "This horse never . . . acted this way . . . until she got . . . ahold of him."

"I know," I had to admit.

"Happens too often," he said, sitting now. "People ruin horses." He tried to get a knee under himself in order to stand, but couldn't quite manage it.

"I wouldn't move if I were you," I advised. "The ambulance is probably on its way."

"I'm not going to wait around for it," he said, making one big gesture with his whole beefy body and managing thereby to stand.

Noel came to inspect him, and he absentmindedly stroked the horse.

"I told Cody to call your next of kin," I said, fishing. "Boots LaRue."

"Very good," he said, dusting off his sleeve. "LaRue *is* my next of kin. He's my brother."

"And the two of you keep selling this one horse."

Standish laughed. Then he said, "Look, it hurts to laugh, so don't make me, all right?"

"But . . . ?" But what had happened?

Standish struggled to move, but he looked as if he owed me an explanation. And sure enough, he started to talk. "You know how hard it is to find a horse that's a true brown," he said. "Like this horse here. Well, my brother found one, an absolute ringer. We were going to switch them out—I mean, you have to agree that the horse was being wasted on Louanne Perry. I mean, even I felt guilty about arranging that—when the ringer colicked and died. You were horse-sitting when we were going to switch them out. We just went ahead and did it anyway."

He shrugged, slowly stood, took two steps, then took two steps backward. He looked up in the sky, as if he were on the deck of a ship and using the stars to get his bearing.

"You came from that away," I said, pointing toward Lola's farmhouse. "Just remember not to run."

I watched him turn and it infuriated me. He was way too cool. All I wanted to do was rattle him. "You know," I said, "you've really cooked it now. Because now there'll be a record of you coming here."

He laughed in a way that said I was wrong. "I came by Learjet. My brother's. I didn't even file a flight plan."

"Wait a minute," I said. "Lest we forget. I know you killed Daisy," I said. "And it was because she was going to sue LaRue. If she had, it would have come out about the horse still being alive." And I'm sure it would have been widely publicized, what with the money Daisy and her husband had spent on the horse. The horse community, after all, isn't that big. Even on a national level. It takes a lot of information to keep all the horse magazines in news. This lawsuit, especially against a name like Boots LaRue, would have been, not just fodder, but a high-calorie feast for them. And Standish would have lost his veterinary license, surely.

Standish stared at me, as if coming to some big decision. "You know it and I know it," he said, "but you don't have any proof. You couldn't even get this brought to trial."

And that was true.

"Just be glad," Standish said, "that I don't sue your friend Lola for all she's worth. This horse is deadly," he said, stroking Noel anew.

I thought he was going to walk away—and it would end right now, right here. In a stalemate.

But, "I'll be back," he said. "One day when you least expect it, I'll be back."

Who did he think he was? Clint Eastwood in one of his early movies, or what?

"You're a jerk," I said.

The horse made nuzzling sounds, as if it were a compliment.

And I couldn't let well enough alone. "Turkey," I shouted as the horse and I watched Standish fade out of sight. At the last minute, he turned and raised his middle finger at us.

Oooh. I wish you could sic horses on people, the way people sic dogs.

I began to wonder just where Cody might be. And then he was striding toward me.

"Standish came to and all of a sudden felt better," I said. "So he left, and we should probably cancel—What's the matter?" I asked him.

"Just great," he said angrily, "come on. Let's get to your place as fast as we can, okay?"

"But we can't run," I reminded him. Noel was standing there watching, but there was no telling what he was planning to do.

Rooney, the pup, was all atwitter, as though wonderful things had been happening and were still going on. His tail, in fact, was wiggling so fast it was a blur; within seconds, the tail started wiggling his whole pup body.

Cody wasn't in the mood for cooing at the puppy, though.

"So are they coming or what?" I asked about the ambulance people, finding Cody's pace somewhere on the border of temptation for Noel.

"Just come on," he said, opening the gate and then standing aside to let me pass through it first.

Remember Teresa? Well, she was standing in the clearing in front of the house. She was holding Jeet's big cast-iron skillet as if it were a baseball bat. She saw me and went, "Ayee," dropping the skillet and covering her face with her hands.

"You see?" Cody was shouting at her, following her movement as though he'd be damned if she'd escape the truth. "Do I look like a robber or a rapist now?"

"Oh, no, no, no." Teresa wept, while Rooney ran in little anticipatory circles, his stump of a tail wagging madly.

"Uh-huh," Cody was saying in an I-told-you-so kind of way. "Uh-huh."

Then, in the distance, we heard an approaching siren.

"The ambulance," I said. "We should have . . . "

"No, no, no," Teresa said, running toward her car.

"Teresa, what's the . . . ?"

Cody was shaking his fist at her. "I told you," he was hollering. "I told you I was with the missus, but no. You couldn't believe me. You couldn't even listen."

Teresa started her engine and began backing up kind of crazily. She rolled the window down and yelled at me: "I am telling your mother about everything."

And then she went roaring off.

And Cody stood there bellowing, "See? See?"

And the next thing I knew, there was a near collision at the gate, with the sheriff's car coming in as Teresa was barreling out.

"It isn't an ambulance," I said, with some petulance, thinking, God, what if we had really needed one?

"I never got that far," Cody said. "The stupid woman thought I was here to get her or something. I ought to have her charged with assault. She hit me on the shoulder with that goddamn frying pan, and . . ."

Well, *somebody* had called the sheriff. Probably Teresa after Cody had fled.

". . . a frying pan is a deadly goddamn weapon," Cody was saying.

But the cavalry was arriving and I had to interrupt him. "We can get the sheriff to arrest Standish," I said.

"Standish is long gone by now," Cody answered. He rubbed his shoulder and stalked toward the sheriff's car just as the siren was winding down. "Don't say anything about him because they'll think you're crazy."

Ha! He could tell them about Teresa and the frying pan, but I'd have to keep my mouth shut or I'd sound crazy! That was a good one! I stepped forward.

"False alarm," Cody was saying, unctuously, as the sheriff's deputy, who looked about twelve, got out. "Maid thought I was a prowler. This is the little lady who lives here," he said, gesturing at me.

I smiled, sort of. As much as I could smile, all told. At the moment I was thinking of what my mother would shortly be hearing from Teresa . . . and then what *I* would be hearing as a result.

"Is that right, ma'am?" the deputy touched the brim of his cowboy hat.

"Yes."

"Maybe we should go inside and sort this out," the deputy suggested.

I opened the kitchen door and gasped. I think I even actually took a step backward.

Cody, in true manful fashion, saw my hesitation and came blundering up behind me to see what the trouble might be.

He, too, was stunned. He, too, I think, made his astonishment known with some gesture.

This raised the deputy's suspicion, and he put a hand on his holster and pushed past both of us.

And there he was, in the middle of—and this is no exaggeration—absolutely the cleanest kitchen I have ever seen with my own eyes, I swear.

Every single surface winked and gleamed. The little chrome things on the stove—the burner pans, I guess—required sunglasses, they were that blinding.

Especially since the room had been smeared with tortilla dough when I'd left it.

"Is everything all right?" the deputy asked. He knew, of course, from our reaction, that it wasn't.

Cody and I nodded sort of dumbly.

Then the telephone rang. Once. Twice. Two more and the machine would pick it up.

"Ma'am?" the deputy said tentatively.

* * *

I lifted the receiver. It was Lola asking questions. Had I seen Cody? Who turned the horse out? What was that siren she'd heard?

I didn't answer any of them. Instead, I countered with questions of my own. "Where were you?" I asked back.

"I went to see *Sense and Sensibility*," she said. "Now it's your turn."

"Cody is right here. And he turned the horse out. And the siren was a false alarm because the maid thought Cody was a prowler."

"The maid? Since when do you have a maid? And why would she think that? Weren't you there to tell her?"

"I can't go into this now," I said. "The sheriff's deputy is still here. But Cody and I will be back because I don't want to stay here by myself tonight." Or actually any night, if you want to know. "We'll just check on Plum and Spier and then I'll drive over."

"Don't wake me up when you get here," Lo said, hammering the phone home.

"I think she's mad," I told Cody.

"Why?"

"Beats me," I said.

The deputy looked puzzled. "Do I need to file a report here on anything?" he asked.

I looked at Cody, hoping that he'd mention Standish and the attempt on my life, but at the same time knowing it wasn't going to happen. For one thing, I wasn't sure that Cody knew about the attempt on my life. But then, why else would he think Standish had been there?

"No," Cody said. "We're got it handled."

* * *

Teresa, despite her present hysteria, seemed to have provided nicely for Plum and Spier. They looked up into the flashlight beam that I shone their way, not even pausing in their hay munching.

Just to be safe, I checked the water trough. It was as full as could be and as clean as the kitchen. I wondered briefly if the horses, stunned by its pristine condition, had refused to drink anything from it.

Louanne Perry should have had Teresa working for her, I realized.

"Okay?" Cody asked, obviously impatient to get back to Lola.

"Yeah." But he looked glum. "I know," I said. "It drives me nuts that Ornell Standish is going to get away with all of this."

"So he admitted it?" Cody asked. "Faking that horse's death?"

"He didn't fake it. They had a horse who looked just like Noel—and they were going to switch them before the ringer horse died. Then they just went and did it anyway."

Cody sighed.

"Well, look," I told him, wheeling Mother down the drive. "If Standish hadn't done all this, Lola wouldn't have Noel, right?"

Rooney, on the seat between us, wriggled as if to emphasize that he was looking at the bright side, too.

"But *does* she have him?" Cody said. "What I mean is, will she be able to keep him?"

"Meaning what?"

"Meaning, won't she have to give him back to Louanne? Even if Standish is never prosecuted, isn't that where he rightfully belongs?"

Rightfully belongs. I wouldn't have suspected anything so noble from the Cody that I used to know. It made me look at him with, well, not new-found respect, because that would imply that I'd only just begun to respect him, but with respect regained after having once flown.

I patted him on the shoulder, and he made a face. I'd picked his sore shoulder, it seemed.

"What?" he said.

"'Oh, we'll think of something," I said.

CHAPTER 15

Lo had said she'd be asleep, but she wasn't. She was in the kitchen, slamming things around the way you do when you're mad but you want the person to ask you about it.

"What's the matter?" I asked.

"Nothing," she said, slamming the silverware drawer.

"You sure?"

Slam. "Yes."

Then Cody walked up to kiss her on the cheek.

This provoked a twist of the head so that he missed. It was followed by yet another slam. She'd had to open one of the cabinets in order to bang it shut, too.

Cody rolled his eyes. For a minute I feared he was going to make a that-time-of-the-month remark—in which case I'd have to kill him.

But he evidently knew that. Whew. He said, "Anytime you want to talk about it . . . " and opened the fridge to get himself a beer.

He offered me one, but I shook my head no.

"Robin doesn't drink beer," Lola snarled. "You'll have to learn these things. She also doesn't eat steak." Slam, slam.

"You don't?" Cody asked me.

"I eat hamburger," I said.

"If I could interrupt for a minute." Lola stepped between us, turning her back on Cody very pointedly.

Rooney danced at her feet, as though some really special event, like a brawl perhaps, were about to happen.

"Isn't he cute?" I said, stooping.

Lola stooped with me. "Your husband left about twenty messages for you on our tape," she said.

"Jeet?"

Lo scoffed. "Of course Jeet. How many husbands do you have? Unless I don't want to know." She stood up and began to walk away.

I followed her. "Well, what did he say?" I asked.

"I don't know," she said. "I erased them."

"You're behaving outrageously," I accused her. "Cody, isn't she?" I looked around, but Cody, probably wisely, had done a fade. "Where'd he go?" I asked.

"I'm not his keeper," Lola said. Then the hostess in her emerged. "You know where the blankets are," she told me, starting back toward the bedroom that she and Cody shared.

I thought, Uh-oh. I had probably done it again, referred to LoCo as Lola's or something. I was forever doing that—cutting Cody out of the picture completely—and Lola was forever getting mad, reminding me that the place belonged to both of them.

"Look, I like Cody," I said, meaning it.

She stood perfectly still, regarding me the way you'd regard, I don't know, a roach before you stepped on it. "I'm certainly glad of that," she said at last. Except she didn't sound glad at all.

I tried to think of a sentence that would include them both, but could only come up with, "Well, good night. To both of you, I mean." At the last minute, I added, weakly, "Merry Christmas."

Lo made a derisive sound. "Merry Christmas," she said pointedly.

Well, excuse me! I thought, Steve Martin–style, as I went into the hall closet to get the blankets she'd mentioned. I tried to think nice thoughts. But basically what I felt was: Here we are, turning ourselves inside out, so she can have a clear title to this horse she's taken a fancy to—and this is how she treats us!

I pulled the blanket down from the top shelf and did a little slamming of my own.

Then I dropped down on the living room sofa, wondering where the puppy had got to. Probably in the bedroom.

The puppy! That was probably what had ticked Lo off. Like, maybe the puppy had chewed something of hers. Or peed again on the floor. Maybe a bunch of times, and she, having just come home from the mall, had had to clean it up, puddle after puddle after puddle of it.

Maybe even more than puddles, maybe piles.

I fell asleep, planning my apology. But heck. She hadn't even been around the puppy much, and anyway, he'd be living at our house come Christmas. That was . . . when? Day after tomorrow? Or the day after that? So what was the big deal?

I must have been dreaming—because the puppy was suddenly 17.2, which is very large for a Jack Russell Terrier. He was chasing Ornell Standish down one of those wide California boulevards.

Standish was running, holding something overhead as if to make absolutely certain that the pup couldn't get to it.

I was somewhere on the sidelines, with Nicholas, who was wearing a Santa suit. There were huge Santa billboards, just like the one I'd seen, only with Nicholas replacing his brother as Santa.

A terrier that was the size of a warmblood was running around the base of one. He stopped and began to chew. The billboard swayed precariously—and a great admonishing finger came out of the sky to wag in the puppy's great big face.

Then a rocket started circling overhead. I watched it going round and round. Then it dived, coming straight at me. Coming with the speed of Noel.

I squinted, attempting to stare it down, and at the penultimate moment, it dropped at my feet. It wasn't a rocket at all; it was a syringe.

I was instantly awake, and even sitting! The syringe! If I could find the syringe that Ornell Standish had dropped, I had him nailed. Because if it contained what I thought it did, I could accuse him of attempted murder!

I flung the blanket back and made my way into Lola's—no, Lola and Cody's—mudroom. I thrashed around until I located the light switch. Then I looked for a flashlight.

Within minutes I was moving through the pasture again, careful not to run because Noel was still somewhere on the premises. I wasn't even sure I could find the exact spot where Standish had appeared with the syringe in hand, but I knew it was over near our gate at Primrose Farm.

I planned to drive it over to Len Reasoner's office.

He'd be able to recognize whatever it was they used to put horses down, which is probably what Standish had been carrying.

I stood near where I thought it had happened and cast the light around. In the darkness, I heard Noel snorting and padding toward me. Not racing toward me, you understand. Just kind of trotting up like a normal horse.

A giant stride forward, I thought. Of course, we'd have to make sure that he still wouldn't try to overtake people who were running, too. But the present progress was heartening—and made his total rehabilitation seem doable.

Of course, I didn't want Noel trampling the syringe, either. And I had to hope that hadn't already happened. Because horses move around a heck of a lot. I don't know if you've ever noticed a paddock after rain, but there will be footprints everywhere. I'm not kidding. It's as though they make it a point to step on every square inch of ground. And this isn't an exaggeration, either.

While all of this was coursing through my mind, the flashlight beam caught something glinting. I approached it, and sure enough, there it was: the syringe—and intact, too.

I picked it up carefully, turned the light off, and headed toward LoCo and my truck.

In less than half an hour. I was in the parking lot outside Len Reasoner's clinic. He had told me once that he always came in at dawn's early light.

So here it was, nearly seven-thirty. Where was he?

But just as I was thinking that, Len's shiny white

pickup rolled into view. I got out of Mother, waving the syringe in the air.

"Tarnation," Len greeted me. "If it isn't the spirit of Christmas herself."

I looked down at my rumpled clothing wondering what he meant. Didn't see anything, though, so I chalked it up to early morning conversation. Meaningless filler. "Hello yourself," I said.

"A fine day, looks like," he said, observing the part of the sky that promised to, within minutes, produce the sun. "Whatcha got there?"

"A potential murder weapon," I said. "No kidding. Ornell Standish was coming for me with it in his hand."

Len narrowed his eyes. "Lemme see that," he said, taking the syringe away.

"Can I go with you?" I asked. "While you analyze the contents?"

"Naw. Because first I've got some animals to tend to. Why don't I just call you when I know."

I wanted to say, *Because I hate to wait for anything,* but I knew that would only prompt a lecture about good manners. "Fine," I said. "Thanks."

"Oh, '*thanks,*' " Len repeated. "Now *there's* a first."

"You be careful," I said teasing him. "That statement comes close to utter rudeness."

Len pretended to shiver as I jumped back in the truck and went home.

Plum and Spier were staring at the house as I drove up. Apparently they hadn't realized that I wasn't inside. Now, however, they whinnied simultaneously before Spier bowed down for a stretch.

Plum spread her hind legs to pee.

I swear, it was almost as though she couldn't eat unless she peed first.

"Okay, okay," I said, walking into the little shed where I kept their grain.

I love this part of the day. Love their expectancy and my ability to satisfy it.

I think all horse owners—or maybe horse keepers, since so many people board their horses out—must feel this way.

I sang "Jingle Bells" as I fed them, feeling good.

Inside, my little answering machine was blinking as if it had a tic. I rewound the tape and turned the volume way up to let the messages boom while I went upstairs to the bathroom.

Jeet. Jeet. Jeet. Then my mother.

Jeet's were all alike, kind of Miss-you, Where-are-you? kinds of things.

My mother's, however, made me edgy. "How could you have borrowed money from Teresa?" she began. "I have repaid her the twenty dollars with interest. And how could you let your kitchen get so vile? And worst of all"—she paused for breath here—"apparently you have a *male friend* who frightened Teresa. I don't know exactly who your *friend* is, or what he had in mind, but I think you ought to—" And then the machine cut off.

My first thought was a fuse.

My next thought—and it came right on the heels of the first—was Ornell Standish again.

Could it be? That he'd come back for a *third* try at me? That he was standing down there in my pristine kitchen . . . probably with mud on his shoes?

I mean, maybe I'm naive, but somehow I thought Noel had knocked some sense into him. And after all, as he'd said when he confessed, I didn't have anything that could actually be used.

I mean, apparently he didn't remember about the syringe.

Sure enough, I heard the floor downstairs make a little creak.

I looked around the bathroom, then grabbed a can of Jeet's shaving cream and went toward the sound.

I waited at the head of the stairs, but the person didn't come up. I listened hard, but there were no more creaks. I began to think fuse again.

I started downstairs, sort of berating myself for leaping to the worst possible conclusion, and, when I almost collided with her, I felt a bolt of terror.

Yes, I said *her*.

Because it was Lola standing there with her arms crossed, as if having waited for me to show up.

"Hi," I said, putting the shaving cream down. "You kind of scared me."

Lo said not a word.

"Did you cut the machine off?" I asked her, walking over to it. "It was my mother. She was talking about Cody, I think. Did you hear the way she kept saying 'friend'? As though it had some big, deep, extra meaning."

Lo didn't answer.

"What's the problem?" I asked her, trying to find the coffee maker so that we could both have some.

I looked in the obvious places, to no avail.

What? Had Teresa stolen it?

"I can't find a thing since Teresa was here." I laughed.

Not a sound from Lo.

"God," I went on. "I need coffee. I assume you do, too," or *you'd have talked by now,* I thought. I mean, I've known Lola for a hundred years; we treat each other like family. I mean, we don't have to pretend anything with each other, pretend to be nice when we aren't feeling nice, et cetera. Usually I think of this as a plus, but today I don't know. Lo was acting pretty weird. "Are you okay?" I asked her.

She made that scoffing sound again. "Sure," she said, but angrily.

"Do you have any idea what could have happened to the coffeepot?" I asked. I was getting more and more ticked as I searched. I mean, what if I managed to find it? I probably wouldn't be able to locate the actual coffee anyway. Except that Jeet ground the coffee himself; there was always a couple of cups worth of residue on the side table where he did it.

Lola cleared her throat kind of pointedly, and I turned to see her gesturing at the coffee maker itself.

"God," I said.

It had been pretty much out in the open, but it was so incredibly clean that it hadn't really registered with me.

Which meant . . . Yes. There was no residue. Even the grinder had been, I don't know what. Scoured or something.

"Jeet is going to think he's in the wrong house," I said.

"I wouldn't be at all surprised," Lola answered. Her voice sounded really nasty. All jagged edges.

"Really," I went on, "I don't think it's ever been like this." I swept a hand in the air to indicate the room.

Lo drew in a huge breath and then started to cry. "How can you rub it in this way?" she said, sobbing. "How can you?"

What? Had she always wanted a maid of her own?

I leaped up and came toward her as she sank into one of the newly polished kitchen chairs. So newly polished that, for a moment, I feared that she'd slide off and crash to the floor. And that was so heavily waxed that she'd probably slide across the floor and crash into the wall, dislodging Jeet's copper-bottomed pots from their roost. They'd fall on Lola's head and . . . Well, of course I was sort of laughing at all of this.

Lola said—or should I say *sniveled*?—"Right. Laugh. Go on. I'm sure you find it very funny."

I came to her side and patted her shoulder. "No," I said, "it isn't that." Meanwhile I was looking frantically around for some Kleenex, but Lord only knows where Teresa would have hidden something like that. "Here," I said, venturing across the room to the paper-towel rack and coming back with a couple of sheets.

Lola took them and began honking into one.

"Lo," I said, "what's the matter?" I mean, I've heard that people get stressed out over the holidays, but I'd never seen Lola quite like this. Except maybe for one time, over Cody! So I said, "It's Cody, isn't it?"

She groaned and honked anew. "I don't get it," she whined. "Don't you care about Jeet at all?"

Talk about a non sequitur. I remembered his messages and said, "I was going to call him back when you came in. I mean, I just haven't had a chance."

"You're going to break it to him over the telephone?" she shrieked, even standing to deliver the line.

I looked at the floor to see if the chair had made a scuff mark. "Break what?" I asked.

"Oh, God. I just can't believe this," she said, pushing past me on her way to the door.

I scooted over to get there ahead of her and barred her from leaving. "Oh, no, you don't," I said. "I'm not letting you out of here until you tell me what's eating you."

Lola stopped crying and drew herself up. Her cheeks had those round red spots I told you about. The ones she gets when she's mad. "You know very well what's eating me," she said. "Your affair with Cody is what's eating me."

I guess my eyes got big and round. They usually do when I'm stunned by something. I know my mouth fell open—and that when I closed it, I gave a great big gulp. "Are you crazy?" I asked her. It was all I could do to keep from reaching up and shaking her by the shoulders.

I did tell you that she was way taller than I am, didn't I? And skinnier, too. And gorgeous.

I mean really gorgeous, with raven black *curly* hair yet.

So why would Cody be interested in me?

"Lola," I said sternly. "Get a hold of yourself. Believe me, I am not having an affair with anyone. *Least* of all Cody." I rolled my eyes and blew a stream of air out to indicate just how impossible that would be.

She cocked her head to the side and narrowed her

eyes at me. She looked like Ava Gardner, and I'd have told her that—except that she didn't share my interest in vintage movies and wouldn't have known who Ava Gardner was. And anyway, this did not seem to be the time to be telling her who she looked like.

"I mean it," I said. "What would make you think such a thing?"

"What would make me think such a thing?" she said, mimicking me. "Well, I don't know. Could it be the way the two of you are always off together? Could it be the conspiratorial way you talk? Could it be that you call the house and ask for *him* and not me, or could it—"

"—be that it's Christmastime and we might be talking about your present?" I suggested.

Of course we weren't, but we could have been. Unless you count making sure that the present she got from Cody wasn't going to be scooped out from under her.

"I already got my present," she said, but the way she said it made me think she only half believed me.

"From Cody you did," I said, "but not from me."

There was a tense moment when we stared at each other. A moment when it could have gone either way. Then, fortunately, Lola started laughing. "Oh, I feel like a moron," she said.

"Well, don't," I said graciously. "But really. Imagine it. Cody and me." I started laughing, too. Until I realized she was back to being miffed. "Now what?" I asked her.

"You've always had it in for him," she said.

"That isn't true," I said, and it wasn't. I started *mistrusting* him after he'd made an ass of himself with Nika Ballinger. But as Jeet once said, quoting some poet, " 'That was in another country and besides, the wench is dead.' " I think it means water under the bridge. And besides, I did find myself warming up to Cody of late, though not in the way Lola had meant at first. But *sheesh*. "What is this? Time-lapse emotions or something? I mean, one minute you're practically accusing me of sleeping with him and the next you're mad because you think I don't like him. Make up your mind."

"You're right," Lola said. "I'm sorry. But I *am* stressed out. But listen, I've got to ask you something. I mean, now that I know you and Cody aren't . . . you know."

"What?"

"Involved," she said. "I need that puppy."

"Huh?"

"The puppy. I want to buy him for Cody," she said. "I mean, Cody is nuts about him."

Are you sure? I wanted to say. *I mean, five minutes ago, you thought he was nuts about me.* Except that I could have been rubbing it in if I'd said that. Plus she was right this time. Cody was crazy about The Macaroon, and I had a feeling that it was mutual.

"I don't know," I said. I mean, he was all I had to give Jeet, considering that I'd spent the money that I had on plane fare to L.A.

"Well," she said, "think about it. Hard. I mean, I'll pay you," she said.

"How much?"

"What do Jack Russells go for?" she asked, inquiring, probably, what I'd paid.

"I don't remember." I lied, thinking that as long as I had to call Louanne about the horse, I might as well give Lola the dog. As a sort of consolation prize. "Take him."

She brightened. "Thanks!" she said.

I watched her go, thinking, *Poor Lo. Little did she know the trade she was going to have to make.*

CHAPTER 16

Although all of the calls I had to make were less than pleasant, I figured I'd get the worst one out of the way, so I called Louanne. And Len Reasoner would have been pleased to note that I began by thanking her again for the pup.

"I'm glad you like him," she said.

"But that really isn't why I called," I admitted. I took a deep breath and launched in. "I don't know how you're going to take this, Louanne," I said, "but I hope you're sitting down. Because I have reason to believe that Wickie is alive. In fact, he's on the farm next door to mine, and he's—"

"Robin," she said, interrupting me. "I know how bad you feel about all of that. But Wickie *is* dead. We'd both rather he weren't, but—"

Now it was my turn to interrupt. "But Louanne—" was all I got out, though.

"My veterinarian says he is," she said. "And frankly, I'm glad."

"You're glad?" I asked. "Glad the horse is dead?"

"No. Glad to be out of horses. Really, Robin. Did I strike you as a horse person?" she asked.

Well, no. "I, uh . . . "

"See what I mean?" she said. "I'm a dog person," she said. "I wouldn't want the horse if he *were* alive.

And anyway, since I collected all that insurance money for him, it would be . . . well, I don't know what. It would probably make them think I'd been out to defraud them or something. So . . . "

"So Wickie is dead," I said.

"Yes."

And long live Noel.

"Merry Christmas," I said.

Then I called Len. And guess what was in the syringe? Succinylcholine.

"What does it do?" I asked him.

"It kills you dead," he said.

"How?"

"Your diaphragm stops working."

"Oh. And how do you spell it?" I asked him.

"I don't know," he said. "I was a phonics baby."

"Well, listen," I said. "Could you hold that syringe? I'll send the Texas Rangers or the sheriff or someone out to get it so it can be dusted for fingerprints."

Len said, "Fingerprints? Girl, are you some kind of insane?"

"What do you mean?" I asked. He'd never talked to me quite this way.

"You should have told me you wanted fingerprints. I've been all over that syringe," he said. "The fingerprints on it are all mine."

Great. So Ornell Standish was going to get away with even this!

Except for one thing. Standish himself didn't know that.

So my next call was to Standish's office. Where I got a recording—with what sounded like The Chipmunks saying that he'd closed for the holidays, that this wonderful time of year was for giving and spending with one's near-and-dear ones. I hung up before they finished, thinking, *Jeet*!

I replayed my messages and got the number Jeet had left. But you guessed it. Jeet was already on his way back to Austin. But wait! It was only the twenty-second. Hadn't he said the twenty-fourth? The night before Christmas? Christmas Eve? God, my husband was coming home and here I was, still dithering around, trying to pin a murder rap on some sleazy vet.

It hardly seemed in keeping with the season.

I called Lola's, Cody answered. I told him that as far as Louanne was concerned, we were in the clear. I also told him what it was that Lola had thought and—I can't say for sure, though, because I couldn't see his face—I swear he was embarrassed. "That's why she's been acting so angry," I explained.

"Angry?" he said. Typical male.

Then I said, "Listen, I don't think Lola should ever know about how this horse is really Wickie."

And Cody said, "I agree." And then he said that Jeet had called—and the three of them, Cody, Lola, and Jeet, had agreed that Jeet would come directly from the airport over there.

"Okay," I said. "I'll feed and be right over."

* * *

Except that I had a brainstorm.

I called Ornell Standish's office again and suffered through all of The Chipmunks this time, and, sure enough, at the end of the message was an emergency phone number, which I tried.

I didn't get him, but the message there gave me his mobile number.

Mentally crossing my fingers, I plugged Jeet's little eavesdropping thing from Radio Shack—well, actually, it's a kind of suction cup that you stick on the phone and you put the other end into a tape recorder so that you can tape whatever the person is saying. In Jeet's use of it, it's logged in probably a million calories in the way of recipes. In my case, I was hoping it would catch a murderer and a thief.

I dialed.

And hey—Ornell Standish actually answered.

I could picture him, tooling around in the wife's BMW roadster, smiling triumphantly when he heard my voice.

Wait, you bastard, I thought. "This is Robin Vaughan," I said. And I thought, evilly to be sure, of Len Reasoner's admonitions lo these many years. "How are you?" I asked. I mean, with a Southernish sort of accent, even.

"Yes?" His voice was impatient and loud. I could hear the whine of traffic behind him, too. "What do you want?" he asked.

I thought of continuing the social chitchat, but I knew I'd lose him. So I got on with it. "The sheriff has the syringe. It has your fingerprints all over it. And he says it was filled with succinylcholine, too." I could only hope I pronounced it right.

"And you think we used that on the ringer," he said disparagingly. "Except we didn't. I keep trying to tell you, the ringer died, the ringer was an accident. We used the ringer, but we didn't kill him."

Okay, okay. "And the woman in Oklahoma," I said, gulping so that the next part of the sentence barely came out, "did you use it on her?"

A laugh. "We did not use succinylcholine on the woman in Oklahoma."

We. "Well," I said, "what did you use?"

No response.

"I said, What did you use?"

"You are unbelievable," Standish said. "Absolutely unbelievable."

"You may not have used succinylcholine on that woman in Oklahoma, but you did try to use it on me," I said. And waited.

Nothing.

"And I've got proof," I said.

"You have a syringe with succinylcholine in it," he said.

"And your prints."

"So what?"

"What do you mean?" I asked. Hadn't he heard me?

"I mean *so what*. I use that stuff every day of the week. So finding a syringe of it with my prints on it means exactly zip."

I thought, *Damn*! Except I said, "Well, the sheriff thought it meant something. He thought it meant you were here. Trying to kill me. And Cody saw the whole thing, too."

"Cody who?"

"Cody, who saw the whole thing." I guessed Standish was unconscious, though, the whole time Cody had been present. "Cody, who went off to call the ambulance. Except that you left before it could arrive." I literally did have my fingers crossed by now.

"Prove it," he said. "I told you, there's no record of my leaving California. You can't prove I was there."

I was trembling all over with frustration. Because this guy had done so much that was wrong. I mean, it was bad enough when I thought he was just out bad-mouthing me, but here he was, a murderer—the murderer of a person and almost the murderer of me—and he was going to get away with it!

Except that I *could* prove he'd left California! Because—remember—Ornell Standish had put a ticket on his Visa, or maybe it was his MasterCard, I couldn't remember. Ha! Screw his brother's Learjet, I had the man! And I said so.

"What are you talking about?" he said.

"I mean, look in your wallet, bozo. Look in your wallet and you'll see that your credit cards are gone. Because I took them. And I charged a ticket from Burbank to here. And so there *is* a record of you coming to Austin after all." I mean, even if the woman at the airport had sold the ticket for cash, someone had come to Austin using his name.

"You *what*?" he said—or rather squeaked and sputtered. I mean—and this was really gratifying—he was *so* upset. "You *what*?" And then the line went first to static and then dead.

So I had the sucker! Sort of. I mean, I didn't really have him in the sense that he would be tried and arrested, but I had him in his head. Let him try to say *So what?* to that!

I went out to hay and grain feeling just great.

* * *

It was still fairly early, so I decided to groom both of the horses before hitting the road for Lola's place. I did Spier first, cross-tying him and getting down my Strongid 2x bucket filled with grooming tools.

Someday there will be a support group for people like me. People who can't throw those plastic Strongid buckets away.

But see, I could think silly things like that now, because I had Ornell Standish by the short hairs. I'd have leaped up and clicked my heels together if I'd known how. I couldn't wait to tell Cody—except that, I'd better not. That's all Lola needed to see was me whispering to him, and I couldn't very well tell Lola, too.

Still, I felt pretty damned satisfied.

In fact, all of my problems seemed solved. Or at least they didn't loom as large. Like I would just have to owe Jeet a present, I thought, since I'd given the one I'd planned for him away.

Now, Lo and Cody could just keep the portrait of Wickie. In fact, that was a fabulous gift. My mother . . . seemed to me I'd already sent her something. Flowers? Well, to be safe I'd send even more. And the animals . . . they'd never know.

I'd managed to do all my shopping, then, without, well, actually shopping. Whew.

Spier seemed to enjoy the feeling of the curry-comb making little circles in his coat. Because he seemed to like it so much, I did it far longer than I ordinarily would have.

Part of me—I mean, face it, grooming, satisfying as it may be, doesn't exactly occupy the mind—was wondering what I was going to get for Christmas, even as I chided myself that my real gifts were Jeet, my wonderful animals, my wonderful friends.

I felt a little puppy pang, though. I would miss The Macaroon. I thought maybe I was ready for another dog after all.

Back at the house, I could hear the telephone start to ring. I would just have to let it. Because no matter how fast I dashed back there, I could never beat the machine.

But I wondered who it might be. If it was my mother, I was glad to be missing the call, because I didn't want to go into the Teresa-Cody squall. And if it was Jeet . . . well, he'd be here soon enough.

Aw, hell, I thought. I'm going to give myself the best Christmas present in the world. In other words, I'd decided to saddle up old Plum and ride.

In fact, I thought, I would ride Plum over to Lola's. The mare could even, I reasoned, spend the night. But then I thought about Spier, back here all alone on Christmas Eve, and I just couldn't do it.

Which is how I ended up riding Plum and ponying Spier, which is to say, bringing him along on a lead line, more or less in tow.

And I went the long way, along the road rather than through the pasture. After all, if there were loose horses out there—and I didn't just mean Noel, I meant *any* loose horse—I didn't want to be riding through.

I don't know about you, but when I'm in the saddle loose horses always make me feel very vulnerable. I mean kneewise and thighwise. I feel, and I guess am, very breakable.

And loose horses always do kind of mill around and act as though they're going to kick. Even if they don't, I want to avoid the minutes of sheer terror.

Maybe I'm an alarmist, I don't know.

But anyway, I went the long way, down the graveled county roads.

And who should come toodling toward me just after I'd left the driveway but my husband.

"Jeet!" I shouted. Except that, although he'd slowed, he didn't stop until he was at least thirty feet past me.

Unless he was preoccupied. But heck. How preoccupied would you have to be to miss a woman—and, not just one but two horses—on the shoulder of the road? A woman who was shouting your name, no less.

Unless he and Lola had conferred when Lo was back in the stage where she thought that Cody and I were carrying on behind her back.

The bitch! I thought.

But no. Jeet was abandoning the car where he'd stopped it and was running back toward me. Which would have been great if the sight of him hadn't upset poor Plum.

Plum started dancing around so that I almost dropped the lead rope that was attached to Spier, which would have meant, great, that we'd have him running around the neighborhood.

But Jeet saw that—I watched him take it in—and he slowed his pace so that the worst case scenario never came to pass. I smiled at him, a trained horse husband now if I'd ever seen one.

"I love you," I said.

"Likewise," he told me.

"So why'd you park down there?"

"Because I want you to be on the ground when you get your Christmas present."

"Ooh," I said, "it's in the car?"

"I'll meet you at LoCo with it," he said.

"What is it?"

"Something you're going to love."

CHAPTER 17

I came up Lola's driveway and spotted her outside, filling the trough in one of the vacant paddocks as if she'd been expecting me.

"Oh," I said, flummoxed. "Did you know I was coming?"

Lo laid the back of her hand against her forehead and looked skyward. "Wanda called," she said.

"She did?" I was impressed.

But, "No, dummy. But Jeet did."

"Oh," I said. "Well, is this okay?" I was belatedly asking whether or not she'd permit the presence of my two horses.

"Sure," she said. She had this goofy expression on her face.

"You know what my present is," I said, tossing Spier's lead rope to her and leaping down from the saddle.

"Yup."

"Oooh," I said, "what?" I ran the stirrup irons up on the near side, while Lo did the same for me on the far.

"I'll never tell," she said, "but he did say he *loved* what you got him."

"Which was . . . ?" I mean, really, I hadn't bought him anything. Not even the purple socks. "No, really. Because I don't even have the puppy to give him now. So what could he mean? Tell me."

"Well, it's not the puppy," she said.

I think she was about to tell me, but Cody came out and yodeled my name. "Did you get my message?" he asked.

"What message?" Lo and I said in tandem.

"Robin," he said, "I called you."

I was undoing the nose cavesson and the throat latch on Plum's bridle. I looked over to see if Lo was making some big deal out of what Cody had just said, but she didn't seem to be. So the storm about our alleged affair was, thank God, over.

Cody came toward us. "Oh, it was something on the five o'clock news," he said. "They'll run it again at ten."

"What?" I said.

"You'll see. It was one of those cutesy holiday things they buy from other stations."

"What kind of cutesy thing?" Lola asked.

"Yeah," I said. "What kind?"

"Oh," he said, "you'll see."

Lola went through the gate with Spier and I followed with Plum. I slid the top of the bridle over Plum's ears and then supported the bit while she expelled it, all froth-covered from her mouth.

Then Lola took the halter off Spier. The two stablemates ambled off amiably to the far end of the paddock in the gathering darkness.

"Maybe we can all go for a ride tomorrow," Lola said.

"Oh, right," I said sarcastically. Chances of Jeet riding were about as good as the chances of really and truly bringing Ornell Standish to justice. And I'd have said so if Lola knew anything at all about what Cody and I had really been up to. But, of course, she never would.

I sighed, and the three of us went back toward the farmhouse.

And that was when Jeet drove up.

"Hey!" I said, running toward the car, but he got out and slammed the door, then held up a hand to fend me off.

"Wait a minute," he said. "I want this to be a surprise."

I turned around and looked at Lola and Cody. He shrugged and Lo looked smug.

Then he opened the car door; we all watched as a Jack Russell puppy gathered its nerve to leap out onto the gravel.

Rooney was brown and white, which I think they call lemon and white, officially. This one was tri-colored. Black, brown, and white. He landed and went along the ground, sniffing.

"He doesn't have a name yet," Jeet said, as I ran toward the puppy and picked him up. Like Rooney, he was all wiggles and licks.

I saw the way Lola and Jeet looked at each other, and I knew right then and there that this had been Lola's idea. She'd probably planned to wrest the other puppy from me the minute she saw him with Cody.

"We're calling our pup something else," Cody said under his breath. "So you can call this one The Macaroon if you want."

"The Macaroon's his name," I shouted. "We can call him Rooney for short." I put him down again;

we all watched him piddle as if it were a performance we'd paid to see.

"What are you calling yours?" Jeet asked.

"I'm curious, too," Lola said, with a skeptical look on her face. "And it better not be Fido."

"It is Fido," Cody said, pretending to pout.

"It's the French version," Jeet suggested. "P-H-I-D-E-A-U-X."

Everyone got a charge out of that one, probably because they were thinking of what I always called the Greek version of flatus, which would be P-H-U-A-R-T.

"By the way, hon"—Jeet put his arms around me—"I love the kitchen. I can't tell you how much I appreciate that. Especially since I know how much you hate to clean." His lips brushed my bangs. "Really, I couldn't have asked for a better present."

"Oh," Lola said, "she just scrubbed and scrubbed and scrubbed. A labor of love."

I was glad I hadn't had time to look for snuggly slippers or purple socks.

At ten o'clock sharp, Cody turned the television on. "They probably aren't going to play it until the end," he said, "but I wanted to be safe."

So we waded through the news and there, at the end, was a fresh-faced man on the screen. It was California, I could tell, with palm trees swaying in the background.

"It was a Christmas tragedy," the commentator was saying. "You might say Santa did it."

"Santa *did* it," I said, thinking of Wanda's eggnogged-drenched prediction. "He didn't bring it."

"Shut up and listen," Cody told me.

"This cheerful billboard," the commentator said—

and on the screen flashed Nicholas's brother in full Santa mode—"became an instrument of death."

Then the camera came to rest on the scene of a wreck. Something huge and flat had indeed just totally crushed an automobile.

The announcer thrust the microphone under a bystander's chin.

"Would you describe the accident?" the commentator asked the witness, a young woman dressed crisply, the way I'd imagine an executive might.

"Well," she said, "the two occupants of the vehicle were driving down the roadway here. The driver was on the telephone. I heard him shouting, 'You *what*? You *what*?'—as though someone on the other end of the line had said something really startling to him. And then he lost control of his vehicle and crashed into the car in front of him—and that car hit another one, and that one rammed into the base of the Santa Claus billboard over there."

"And then it . . . " the commentator prompted.

"And then it fell on top of the vehicle that you see over there and smashed it. It was one of those new BMW roadsters, too."

Then the camera was back on the commentator. "Both of the occupants of the roadster"—he glanced at his notes—"a Nimrod LaRue of Houston, and an Ornett . . . er . . . an Ornell Standish of Burbank, were killed in this freak holiday accident."

"Nimrod LaRue!" Lo shouted. "That's Boots LaRue. The horse dealer." She knew him, of course, being a horse dealer of sorts herself. "God, what a loss!"

Cody and I exchanged a look.

"Gee, old Boots LaRue," Lola was saying, shaking her head.

And me, I was thinking of my last conversation with the unfortunate Ornell Standish. Wherein he'd shouted exactly the words that the executive woman remembered hearing before the crash. "You *what*? You *what*?" I was thinking of the not very Christmas-y notion of karma.

The newscast, meanwhile, had gone from the on-the-street film to the studio with the anchor team.

"Say," one of the anchors asked, "did you find out anything about who the victim of that freak accident was talking to?"

My heart stopped. Especially when Cody turned around to stare as if he knew that it had to have been me.

The commentator shuffled through his notes and then said, "Nope. Couldn't come up with it."

Whew.

Cody reached for the remote.

"Oh, wait," Lola said, jumping up. "Let me show you the video we made this afternoon." Two Jack Russell puppies thundered past, and Lo all but stumbled over them. Then she popped a cassette into the VCR and we were watching Lo out in the pasture with Noel.

She came in, carrot in hand, and Noel approached at a walk. Then, while he was eating, she walked part of the way away, then skipped a few paces, looking over her shoulder.

Nada.

She approached the camera. "I still have to keep my eye on him," she said. "But basically, he's as safe as any other horse on the property."

She turned the VCR off and the tape popped out.

"Good job," I told her.

"Oh, he's the best," she said. "Really. The best

Christmas present I could have ever hoped for. He's fabulous. He's . . . " She paused, trying to think of a superlative that would mean something. "To die for."

And the scholar in Jeet emerged. "Where did an expression like that come from anyway?" he asked. "Why can't we say a horse 'to treasure,' or a horse 'to love,' or a horse 'to enjoy'? What does 'to die for' mean, anyway?"

"Beats me," I said, snatching up one of the Christmas pups.

DEATH BY DRESSAGE

Nika Ballinger has only a rich husband to mourn her violent death, which appears to be murder. As fellow horsewoman Robin Vaughan mounts her own search for the killer, she rummages through Nika's untidy past and finds a bizarre double life that someone might kill to keep secret.

GROOMED FOR DEATH

Equestrienne Robin Vaughan and her food critic husband Jeet travel to New York City, where Robin runs into trouble at a Central Park stable—not to mention a grisly murder.

MURDER WELL-BRED

On the heels of a disastrous interview with a famous dressage master, Robin runs into an old friend who later turns up dead. Wild horses couldn't keep Robin from snooping for the truth, a story too bizarre to believe and much too dangerous to print.

DEATH ON THE DIAGONAL

When Robin and Jeet arrive in their new home of Bead, Texas, the most exciting event is the yard-of-the-week competition. Until Robin begins to investigate a hit-and-run death and uncovers too many secrets best left buried.